I0638033

The Case of Cosmic Chaos

Volume 14 of

The Casebooks

Of Octavius Bear

Harry DeMaio

"Alternative Universe Mysteries for Adult Animal

Lovers"

THE CASEBOOKS OF OCTAVIUS BEAR

Paperback ISBN 978-1-78705-768-5
ePub ISBN 978-1-78705-769-2
PDF ISBN 978-1-78705-770-8

Published in the UK by MX Publishing
335 Princess Park Manor, Royal Drive,
London, N11 3GX
www.mxpublishing.com

Cover layout and construction by
Brian Belanger

Dedicated to GTP

A Most Extraordinary Bear

And to the late Ms. Woof

An Extremely Sweet and Loving

Dog

Acknowledgements

These books have evolved over a long period of time and under a wide range of influences and circumstances. I am indebted to many people for helping to bring Octavius and his cohorts to the printed and electronic page. Thanks most especially to my wife, Virginia, for her insights and clever suggestions as well as her unfailing enthusiasm for the project and patience with its author.

To my sons, Mark and Andrew and their spouses, Cindy and Lorraine, for helping to make these tomes more readable and audience friendly. To Cathy Hartnett, cheerleader-extraordinaire for her eagerness to see this alternate universe take form. To Jack Magan, Paul Bernish, David Chamberlain, Dan Walker, Dan Andriacco, Amy Thomas, Luke Benjamin Kuhns, David Marcum, Derrick Belanger, Gretchen Altabef and Zohreh Zand for their enthusiastic encouragement. And to all of my generous Kickstarter backers.

Kudos to Jim Effler, the late Bob Gibson and Brian Belanger for their wonderful illustrations and covers. Thanks, of course, to Sharon, Steve and Timi Emecz at MX Publishing for giving The Great Bear and his gang of Octavians a great home.

If, in spite of all this support, some errors or inconsistencies have crept through, the buck stops here. Needless to say, all of the characters, situations, and narratives are fictional. Some locations, devices, historical figures and events are real.

Also by Harry DeMaio

The Octavius Bear Series – Books 1 to 13

1-The Open and Shut Case

2-The Case of the Spotted Band

3-The Case of Scotch

4-The Lower Case

5-The Curse of the Mummy's Case

6-The Attaché Case

7-The Suit Case

8-The Crank Case

9-The Basket Case

10-The Camera Case

11-The Wurst Case Scenario

12-The Nut Case

13-A Case of Déjà Vu

Note to the Reader:

The Casebooks of Octavius Bear are designed to be read individually, independently and in any order. That is why some preliminary information is repeated in each volume.

This book is no exception. However, you may get a fuller understanding of some of the dynamics and characters in this Volume 14 if you have already read Volume 13 – A Case of Déjà Vu. Not necessary, mind you. Just a suggestion.

In any event, I hope you enjoy this story. Thanks for taking it up.

The Development of Civilization Volume 14 Part 1

Our Origins

From "An Introduction to Faunapology"
by Octavius Bear Ph.D.

About 100,000 years ago, according to scientific experts, a colossal solar flare blasted out from our Sun, creating gigantic magnetic storms here on Earth. These highly charged electrical tempests caused startling physical and psychological imbalances in the then population of our world. The complete nervous systems of some species were totally destroyed. For example, "Homo Sapiens" lost all mental and motor capabilities and rapidly became extinct. Less developed species exposed to the radiation were affected differently. Four-footed and finned mammals, birds and reptiles suddenly found themselves capable of complex thought, enhanced emotions, self-awareness, social consciousness and the ability to communicate, sometimes orally, sometimes telepathically, often both. Both speech production and speech perception slowly progressed with the evolution of tongues, lips, vocal cords and enhanced ear to brain connections. Many species developed opposable digits, fingers or claws, further accelerating civilized progress. Some others (most fish and underground dwellers) were shielded from radiation and remained only as sentient as they were before the blast. This event is referred to as The Big Shock. It remains under intensive study.

Positive in our knowledge that we are not alone in the cosmos, my staff and I are heavily engaged in Project Multiverse, successful searches for alternate universes, especially those in which "Homo Sapiens" continues to live and hopefully, prospers. This book presents some of the results of that project.

The Players

- **Octavius Bear** – Mega-sized Kodiak; Narcoleptic war hero; Consulting Detective; Scientist; Inventor; Seeker of Justice; Gazillionaire owner of Universal Ursine Industries; Gourmet/Gourmand; Bee Keeper; Somewhat sedentary and grouchy just on general principles.
- **Mauritius (Maury) Meerkat** – Narrator; Assistant to Octavius; Theatrical Agent; African *émigré* with a French-Dutch background; clever with a shady history.
- **Bearoness Belinda Béarnaise Bruin Bear** *(nee Black)* – Gorgeous polar superstar with the Aquashow, ***"Some Like It Cold;"*** Wife of Octavius; Extremely rich widow of Bearon Byron Bruin living part time in Polar Paradise in the Shetlands; Owner-pilot of the last flying Concorde SST.
- **Arabella Bear** – Hybrid bear cub prodigy; Twin daughter of Bearoness Belinda and Octavius.
- **McTavish Bear** – Hybrid bear cub prodigy; Twin son of Bearoness Belinda and Octavius.
- **Mlle Woof** – Bichon Frisé – Governess to the twin cubs.
- **Frau Schuylkill** – Octavius' beautiful Swiss she-wolf estate manager/cook/pilot/security officer with many other mysterious and military talents. She rescued Octavius from his dive off the Breakurbach Falls while he was struggling with his nemesis, Imperius Drake.
- **Wyatt Where** – The Colonel – Another wolf; Former military intelligence officer who had retired to a security post at the Bank of Lake Michigan in Chicago and then quit to join Octavius; Mate to Frau Schuylkill.
- **Howard Watt** – Porcupine; High tech security authority who also left the Bank to join Octavius; Alternate Universe specialist; Laser and particle beam accelerator expert.
- **Marlin** – Dolphin (sic) – the Prince of Whales' Chief Scientist; Magician and part time Jester; Howard's Multiverse associate.
- **Otto the Magnificent – aka Hairy Otter** – An absolutely terrible illusionist magician, Otto the Magnificent escaped the claws of super villain Imperius Drake but not before he developed some amazing powers courtesy of Imperius' genetic alterations.
- **L. Condor** – Andean Condor; cybernet genius with a twelve-foot wingspan and artificial voice. Newly appointed Chief Technical Officer (CTO) of the Advanced Super Computing Center UUI. (The Hexagon)
- **Chita** – Beautiful, fascinating, clever, sexy, immoral and highly independent feline who among other things, is the publisher and editor-in-chief of *PURR* and *SOW* magazines.

- **Lord David** – Dalmatian Dog – Chamberlain to the Exiled King.
- **Dancing Dan** – Boxer – Lord David's Bodyguard and Personal Trainer.
- **Jaguar Jack the Lad** – Longtime Compadre of Octavius Bear.
- **Chief Inspector Bruce Wallaroo** – Irrepressible but brilliant marsupial; an international law and order genius from Down Under; currently assigned to Interpol; often calls on Octavius and Maury for support.
- **Caleb Cassowary** – Former Chief Technical Officer (CTO) – Advanced Super Computing Center-UUI. Now a fugitive in the Multiverse.
- **Byzz – Byzantia Bonobo** – Brilliant Assistant and collaborator to Caleb.
- **Dougal** – Shetland Sheep Dog – Estate Manager of Polar Paradise.
- **Ms. Fairbearn** – Canadian Polar – Chief Housekeeper of Bearmoral Castle / Polar Paradise.
- **Bearmoral Shetland Sheep: Dolly, Holly, Molly and Polly** – Housemaids, Lounge Waitresses and probable Clones.
- **Mrs. McRadish** – Sheep – Chief Cook at Polar Paradise.
- **Fiona** – Dandie Dinmont Terrier – Lounge Manager at Polar Paradise.
- **Lion and Unicorn** – Proprietors of the Baltasound pub of the same name.
- **Harold** – Sea Otter in charge of the castle's beaches, pools and watercraft.
- **The Prince of Whales** – UK Undersea Royalty,
- **Benedict and Galatea Tigris** – Siblings; White Bengal Tigers; Pilots of Belinda's and Octavius' aircraft; The Flying Tigers.
- **Wolford Wolverine** – UUI and Octavius' personal Lawyer,
- **Preston Pavel Polar** – Ursine Movie Star, Director.
- **Bree** – Ursine Movie Ingenue.
- **Herr Gustav Schäferhund** – German Shepherd – Movie Producer.
- **Doris and Ella** – Grizzly Bears – Movie Production Assistants.
- **Sheldon and Seymour** – The Racoon Brothers – Scriptwriters.
- **Lukas Lynx** – Cinematographer.
- **Ursulas 12&13** – Universal Ursine Intellects – Artificial General Intelligence Systems.
- **Huntley** – Siberian Husky – Bear's Lair Butler.
- **Doctor "Odd" Vark** – Chief Geneticist at Universal Ursine Industries.
- **Special Agent Honey Badger** – FBI.
- **Flame** – An Extraordinary Fire Engine.

Locations

Cincinnati, Ohio; UUI, and the Hexagon, Kentucky; Bearmoral Castle/Polar Paradise, the Shetlands; and Alternate Universes

Octavius

Prologue

Do Bears give you a scare? Well, me too.
So, I'll pass on this tactic to you.
You just fix that old Bear
With a cold, piercing stare.
But make sure that he's Winnie-the-Pooh.

Hello again or first-time greetings to new readers of the Casebooks of Octavius Bear. I am Mauritius (Maury) Meerkat, sidekick to Octavius Bear and your genial host and narrator. Delighted to welcome you to Volume Fourteen – *The Case of Cosmic Chaos.* After the close of our last adventure *A Case of Deja Vu (Book 13)* the Octavians staged a mass exodus on the huge C-5A Ursa Major from the Bear's Lair in Cincinnati to escape the recent nonsense and get a little R&R. Off to Bearmoral Castle/Polar Paradise here in the Shetlands.

Octavius and I; our two magnificent Wolf associates, Frau Schuylkill and Colonel Wyatt Where; and our resident all-round talent, Otto the Magnificent are all present and accounted for. Readers of Book 13 will realize that L. Condor (Condo) is now the Chief Technical Officer (CTO) – Advanced Super Computing Center-UUI. He's back in Kentucky at the huge Hexagon, cleaning up the mess left by Caleb Cassowary, the former CTO and now alternate-universe fugitive along with his assistant Byzantia Bonobo. We're not sure where they are but it's not Earth.

Our scientific geniuses Howard Watt and Marlin the Dolphin are at the Bear's Lair running our Multiverse Project. Our newly hired Butler, Huntley Husky is also holding down the fort in Cincinnati.

We also have a few special guests and new members of the Octavians with us. Lord David – a Dalmatian Dog – former Chamberlain to the now deceased exiled King of Dalmatia and Dancing Dan Walker – a Boxer – Lord David's Bodyguard and Personal Trainer. Lord David has a wonderful fire engine, Flame, that he has brought to the resort on the C-5A and utility helicopter as he and Dan take on the job of Polar Paradise Security. The Cubs are crazy about the truck. Rounding out the cast of characters is Jaguar Jack the Lad – longtime compadre of Octavius Bear. Missing at the moment are Chita and Bruce Wallaroo. Fear not. They'll appear!

We have taken up residence at the palatial resort after celebrating back at the Bear's Lair in Cincinnati, the fourth birthdays of Belinda and Octavius' super-precocious twin Cubs, Arabella and McTavish.

We're awaiting the arrival of Octavius' wife, Bearoness Belinda Béarnaise Bruin Bear *(nee Black)* here at Polar Paradise, her Shetlands Castle/Resort and part time home. She's flying with the Cubs separately via the Aquabear, the last SST Concorde aloft. On this run, the plane is piloted by Benedict and Galatea Tigris, the Flying Tigers, twin sibling white Bengals.

Belinda, in order to retain her Bearonial status, must occupy the castle at least six months of the year. She and Octavius do high speed commutes between their spectacular homes in Cincinnati and Scotland. Today, she is accompanied by Chita, the Cubs and their governess, Mlle Woof. You will meet the Fabulous Furballs, shortly.

As I said, my name is Maury Meerkat – also known as Offscreen Narrator. When I am part of the action, I am Octavius' trusted associate and field captain. I am two feet tall plus tail and I weigh in at twenty-four pounds. He, on the other hand, is a huge Kodiak – over nine feet tall and 1400 pounds – and like many of his species, given to emotional outbursts.

As you may already know, Octavius prides himself on his many skills in the fields of biology, physics, ursinology, voodoo, teleology, chemistry, apiculture, and oenology. He is a self-made gazillionaire and still sole owner of UUI *(Universal Ursine Industries.)* He is also a first rate electrical, electronic, structural, marine, computer, communications, aeronautical, civil, mechanical, aerospace and chemical engineer. He has a few other interesting characteristics such as falling into brief, deep narcoleptic comas – side effects of his successful genetic experiments to eliminate the need for him to hibernate.

However, the talent and occupation that should interest you most is his avocation for criminology. The Bear works in close concert with Inspector Bruce Wallaroo from Australia and Interpol, of whom more later, and with his own Cincinnati and Shetlands based team – The Octavians:

When we are not out scouring the world for evildoers, in cooperation with local, national and international constabularies, we are primarily headquartered in a rambling old mansion near Cincinnati which encompasses not only the Great Bear's opulent digs, but his massive laboratories and shops; his missile silo disguised as an Asian pagoda; *(Don't ask!)* and a giant Roman temple that serves as a hangar for his four airplanes: a Twin Otter; a F15E Strike Eagle; a V-22 Osprey; a C5A-The Ursa Major; plus an AgustaWestland AW101 VVIP luxury helicopter -The Ursa Minor. Why so many? Ask him!

Across the Ohio River in Northern Kentucky, sit the headquarters, labs and some production facilities of UUI. (Universal Ursine Industries) Further west is the fantastic Deep Data Hexagon, home of the UUI Advanced Super Computing Center. Our story will take us back there periodically.

Now let me take a moment and further introduce a highly essential and near-miraculous member of the Octavians - Ursula 12 – Universal Ursine Intellect Model 12– Artificial General Intelligence System (AGI.) I'll let Ursula 12 explain herself.

"Thank you, Maury. Hello everyone!! My official nomenclature is Universal Ursine Intellect Model 12 – Artificial General Intelligence System. Ursula 12 for short. My predecessor systems were developed by the Advanced Super Computing Center at UUI. I am the result of the Computing Center team using those earlier versions to create a further enhanced entity - me, the Model 12, which, we hope will help produce even more sophisticated, independent and powerful AGI systems (the Model 13) in the future. Each advanced unit contains the capabilities, memories and power of its progenitors so in a sense, we are not replacing but rather expanding the Ursula family."

"While I am physically supported by a highly secure and hyper-powered server farm at the Kentucky Deep Data Hexagon, I also exist independently in clouds and network-based nodes and can be simultaneously incorporated into a wide variety of separate devices like this laptop unit. I combine quantum computing elements with extremely high speed conventional circuits. I have practically limitless data capacity and 5G+ transmission speed. My super high-velocity multi-tasking abilities allow me to continuously serve an exceptionally large number of entities while simultaneously and autonomously enhancing my own abilities."

"Depending on the physical unit in which I'm housed, I can see, hear, feel and smell. I speak and understand an almost infinite number of languages and dialects. I can change my appearance and my vocal output to suit most moods and situations. I can interact with other devices, vehicles and structures and of course, all varieties of sentient animals in this world."

"I am also an important component of the Multiverse Project and am adapting my capabilities to deal with alternate universes as they are discovered. I have restraining functions which prevent me from doing deliberate harm even in self-defense, unless I am released by a recognized authority using very carefully protected clandestine codes. Finally, I have been told that although the Model 12 is shy on emotions, I have developed a finely-honed sense of humor. LOL!"

Ursula has other highly important capabilities that we don't talk about publicly such as breaking all known encryption codes and piercing deep personal identification techniques.

Our team no longer believes she is magical or supernatural. I'm not sure what she is. Her personality gets more independent and socially adept every day and she has taken to anticipating our interactions with ease and accuracy. Needless to say, for security purposes, we conceal her existence to all but a very few individuals with a need to know. She is also highly skilled in self-protection.

With the disappearance of Caleb and Byzz from the Hexagon, it is not clear if and when Ursula 13 will be developed. The Ursulas were their babies, especially Byzantia. Now, that's up to Condo to manage. Meanwhile Ursula 12 is very much in control. Stay tuned.

*****

The air was suddenly filled with the screams and roars of jet engines. *(or was it the Cubs?)* The Aquabear SST had arrived at Abeardeen Airport and with it The Bearoness, Chita, the Cubs and their governess, Mlle Woof, a small but highly competent Bichon Frisé. The Bearoness typically pilots the Concorde but this time the all-white Flying Tigers whom I neglected to include in my introductions landed the Aquabear and finessed it into position in front of a huge ice blue and white hangar decorated with a portrait of Belinda in Bearonial raiment.

That aircraft has been doing yeoman duty shuttling Octavian players hither and yon and reducing the size of the Bear's fabulous wealth in the process. Operating and maintaining the Ursine Air Force is a major financial drain but neither Octavius nor Belinda will hear of reducing or stinting on the expense. I recently got a raise so who am I to complain.

The ground crew rolled the airstairs up to the passenger exit and promptly got out of the way. Out the door shot Arabella and McTavish, the Cubs, racing toward the shuttle helicopters. "C'mon Momma, C'mon Mlle Woof, C'mon Aunt Chita. Let's go to Polar Paradise."

Three females serenely descended the stairs - Belinda, Chita and Mlle Woof. Octavius, who had ridden the shuttle down to Abeardeen to greet them gave the Bearoness a welcoming hug. Mlle Woof immediately fell into corralling the Cubs.

"Welcome ladies. How was your flight?"

Belinda smiled. "Rough even at 60,000 feet. Glad the Tigers were doing the flying. Chita wasn't at all happy with the turbulence and of course, the Cubs can turn any ordinary airplane ride into a major escapade. They're still on a high from their birthdays and success with their electronic game. The Bold Brave Brilliant Bumptious Bears tournaments for the Internet. They already have over a million users signed up. They're in the Clouds – literally."

The ground crew transferred their luggage to the shuttle chopper. They sedately settled themselves in for the one hour plus trip to the Polar Paradise. All except the cubs, of course, whose noise matched the whirlybird's engines.

"Poppa, is Uncle Davey, Dan and Flame *(the fire truck)* at the Castle?"

"Yes, they are! Flame came up on the large utility helicopter."

"What about Uncle Jack?"

"He's up there too, although he's not going to spend too much time with us. He left his car in Cincinnati at the Bear's Lair. He has to go back to the Hexagon where they're working on his horse racing betting systems. Senhor Condor restored his development team that Caleb had taken away."

"What happened to Caleb and his assistant?"

"We're not sure. They fled on a Multiverse trip but we don't know where. Marlin and Howard are trying to track them down. Half the world wants to get their paws on them. They caused a lot of damage."

"He was a bad guy!"

"He still is. We need to get them back before he causes more trouble."

Arabella's eyes widened. "Are we in danger, Poppa?"

"I don't think so, Bella. The Frau and Colonel are with us and so is Uncle Davey and Dan but I'd feel a lot better knowing Caleb was in jail somewhere here on Earth. Don't worry. We'll find them."

McTavish piped up. " I don't get it Poppa. What was Caleb trying to do and why was he doing it?"

"He wanted to take over UUI and get rid of us. I wasn't going to stand for that. He made quite a mess but we've got most of it cleaned up. As to why, he believes he's superior to all other animals and should be absolutely in charge of everything. I'm not going to stand for that either. When we find him and his assistant, they're going to spend a long time in prison. A lot of animals want to get their paws and claws on them. Right now, they're somewhere in the Multiverse. It's a big place but we'll get them."

Arabella grinned. "Can we use them in our game?"

Belinda snorted, "Definitely not! If I hear that you've done that, your game playing will be over permanently. Is that clear?"

"Awww!!"

On to Polar Paradise and one of Mrs. McRadish's sumptuous meals. By tacit agreement, Frau Schuylkill kept out of the kitchens while she was at the castle. They were the province of a lovely sheep chef whose gastronomic skills were hailed by all the tourists and staff. None of this Haggis stuff for Mrs. McRadish. She was an international culinary professional of the first rank and our Cordon Bleu she-wolf respected her. A She-wolf and Sheep who got along by staying out of each other's way and kitchen. Remarkable!

Another notable Shetlands success story was Ms. Phoebe Fairbearn, a Canadian Polar – restored as Chief Housekeeper of Bearmoral Castle / Polar Paradise. Her son Algernon was the malicious villain in our story, *(The Crank*

Case Volume Eight) and she had a dreadful marriage to Jack DeLad, a nasty grizzly bear criminal. Belinda, Fetlock Holmes and Octavius managed to save Phoebe from prosecution for hiding and protecting her son. They assisted her in divorcing her shiftless husband while preserving her job as Chief Housekeeper. Needless to say, her loyalty and gratitude are immense. Among them, she, Mrs. McRadish and Dougal keep Polar Paradise at a superb level of comfort, service, cleanliness and general enjoyment. The Castle celebrates the highest holidaymaker travel reviews.

Years ago, the Castle began life as a hundred-room hotel, spa and open sea swim resort. It did well but the original Bearon's other investments did even better and by the time he died, his arrogant son and daughter decided the Castle should be converted into a sumptuous residence suitable for bears of breeding, *(dubious)* stature, *(unremarkable)* history, *(fake)* and wealth, *(real.)*"

Down came the cutesy neon signs of cuddly polar cubs and up went the heraldic banners along with a mass importation of phony clan symbols, tartans, weapons and other status conscious folderol. Belinda thought the whole thing was a big hoot and just enjoyed the place for what it was. Most of the locals who know Bel are fond of her and admire her but in general the Bruin "clan" was not very much liked. Good riddance when they left! If it weren't for Belinda's generosity and social conscience, all of the Bearmoral Castle riches would still be locked underneath the moat.

The waters of the North Sea and Atlantic provide an ideal venue for vacationing Polar Bears from Canada and the Bering Sea. Prior to its reconversion into a resort hotel, Bearmoral Castle, as it was then called, was the home of the now deceased Bearon Byron Bruin, shady first husband of Bearoness Belinda. He was killed in an avalanche filming a Pola Cola commercial. Unfortunately, it was also home to his relatives; a bigger group of snobbish undesirables from the Bering Sea would be hard to imagine. Turns out, they were a bunch of criminal phonies and were tossed out by Belinda. She turned the castle back into the resort it had once been, only much more so. It keeps improving and attracting more and more ursine and non-ursine tourists.

Today, much of the Scots décor has been preserved but updated with a "now" look. In fact, the new resort bodes well for the economy and more jobs throughout the Shetlands. The moat has been totally cleaned out, refilled with circulating water, and local seals and otters were hired to perform in it several times a day, weather permitting. A functioning drawbridge that gets pulled up at night is also a major tourist attraction. Some of the original signage was salvaged and new electric and electronic glitz installed.

So, the Castle has been restored to its original resort status along with several new additions. With the departure *(hasty but complete)* of the "family," Belinda speeded up the timetable to turn the castle back into the fun place the first Bearon had in mind. *Polar Paradise* has again become the luxury playground destination of choice for the northern ursines and for other chill-seeking populations. However, for those of us who come from warmer climes, there are several spas and saunas.

The beach itself has been upgraded and several different forms of sea craft as well as a floating dock have been added for the frigid water loving guests. *(Not me!)* All under the management of Harold, a sea otter.

The castle's theatre and ballrooms have been taken out of mothballs and the indoor pool has been refurbished to do double duty as a show venue. The castle is also the home of the world famous Aquabears, an aquatic show team combining synchronized swimming, high diving and high jinks into a spectacular performance experience.

The prima water ballet, diving, and synchronized swimming star of the long running Aquashow, "Some Like it Cold," Belinda combines all the coy *hauteur* of a super wealthy diva and the glitzy horsepower of the best of the showbiz superstars There is now year-round entertainment, including, of course, the Aquabears. Belinda only occasionally joins the group and Otto, with his telekinetic talents, provides comic relief with slapstick antics. He has other more serious capabilities which we will soon illustrate.

Octavius Bear uses the Castle as his auxiliary base as we shall see in the following tale. A Genetic Research Institute is also housed within its walls.

Transportation from mainland Scotland and Abeardeen is provided by helicopter and ferry service. A constant stream of whirlybirds descends on a helipad in the castle's expanded courtyard. Non-flyers come in after a longer but luxurious sea voyage. Right now, it is high season at Polar Paradise.

The Castle was also the site of several swashbuckling films made by the Russian superstar Preston Pavel Polar. *(See Book 10 – The Camera Case)* Belinda, Octavius and the Cubs all had walk-on roles.

It's a not too carefully guarded secret that I am also a talent agent with most of the Octavians as my showbiz clients. I started with Otto but expanded my services to the others. It keeps me busy. My talent agency work is flourishing, but I have to be careful not to rock the boat with Octavius. Truth be told, while I enjoy show biz, my heart still chases the ne'er-do-wells.

Now missing from the Scottish climes are two lovely Polar twins. Bearnice and Bearyl Blanc. These ladies, a singer and actress respectively were also the pilots of Belinda's SST. They both have very active and highly successful show careers. They too starred in Preston's extravaganzas.

The other passenger on the latest Concorde flight was Chita. She is a very complex individual. A former associate of the arch-criminal Imperius Drake, she had a serious falling out with him. *(He tried to kill her but she got him first.)* She has since gone straight, joined the Octavians and is often engaged in our more sensational adventures.

She edits and publishes two magazines, several social media and TV outlets and a few other publications. She occasionally reverts to one of her early vocations – modeling. Like all of her cheetah counterparts, she has spectacular legs. She adds a sensuous strut and a major case of attitude to help the image along. Oh yes, I forgot. She's also a singer. She was a member of the now defunct Spotted Band. (See Book Two of the same name) All told, she's "fahbulous, dahling."

A little later, I'll give you more insight into Frau Schuylkill and her mate, Colonel (ret.) Wyatt Where. Also Doctor Howard Watt and Marlin, the Dolphin. You will meet all these worthies as we spin through these pages. Stay with us.

Now, let us go to the Castle's Lion and Unicorn Lounge where post luncheon relaxation is the order of business.

Bearoness Belinda
Béarnaise Bruin
(nee Black)

Chapter One

The Octavians sit for a drink.
Jaguar Jack joins the group with a wink.
They arrange for a run
That will be lots of fun
Lion and Unicorn's Pub! Don't you think?

(Polar Paradise)

After lunch, Belinda and Chita each held a bubbling champagne bowl in their paws as they took up seats among the tourists in the Lion and Unicorn Lounge managed by Fiona, the Dandie Dinmont Terrier.

The Colonel and Frau Schuylkill, Otto and I had arrived earlier and once again Otto was regaling Ms. Catt with stories of intergalactic adventures. Accent on the missing ex-CTO and his assistant.

Chita shivered. She has an aversion to Multiverse activity and had shaken off all invitations to participate in Quantum travel. "I'll stay in this world, if you don't mind!"

The Colonel, himself an alternate universe traveler, laughed. "You don't know what you're missing, Chita. Literally! Three moons in the sky. Non-stop sunsets! Endless forests and waterfalls! Philosopher gophers!"

"Yeah and nutty birds set on world conquest. No thanks!"

"We've got them here on Earth, too. Witness our Cassowary friend."

"Yeah, I know. Belinda, have you and the Cubs ever gone off on an interplanetary jaunt?"

"Not exactly. Our trip to Egypt came close as did yours, Chita. *(See Book 5-The Curse of the Mummy's Case.)* That awful Pharaoh was other-worldly enough for me, thanks."

"How about you, Maury?"

"Yep, been there, done that as has Octavius."

The Great Bear had been out of the room and returned with his cask of mead and an Ursula 12 laptop firmly in paw. "What have I done?"

"Taken Multiverse journeys."

"Yes, we've done that and intend to do more, don't we Ursula?"

"Oh, certainly, Doctor Bear, any time. Especially if we need to nab Caleb."

"Where are our guests?"

"Jaguar Jack and the Cubs are out looking over Flame, the fire engine owned by the Dalmatian Lord Chamberlain, *(now known as Uncle Davey)*. Dancing Dan, his retired professional Boxer bodyguard / trainer is with them."

"That truck seems to be his pride and joy."

"Oh, indeed. You couldn't get him to part with it. A gift from his Majesty, the late Dalmatian King. They took the Cubs for a couple of rides and let them sound the bells and siren. Friends forever! And now, they're going to head up the Polar Paradise Fire Department and Security Office."

"Well," said Belinda, "We certainly needed one and I'm glad we could find a home for Lord David and Dan."

"They seem happy."

"And secure, now that Ursula and the Frau tracked down the Croatian assassins who were after them. Oh, here comes Jack."

"Hola, Señores, Señorinas and Señoritas. Where can a thirsty Jaguar find a bowl or two of Tequila?"

Fiona barked, wagged her tail and invited the spotted cat to sit. A few moments later she emerged from behind the extended bar with a tray supporting several bottles of pure Agave nectar, a bowl and dish of salt.

"Señorita Fiona, you are a jewel of great price. To find such liquid Mexican riches in the land of Scotch whisky is indeed a miracle."

"Oh, Señor Jack, you must go to the village and visit Lion and Unicorn. They have a treasure trove of fine liquors and wines."

The Great Bear agreed. "They have some of the finest mead in the world. Almost as good as mine. You'll love those two. But be careful of mistaken identification. There was a no-good Grizzly called Jack DeLad who was captured there by the Police. Our poor Chief Housekeeper, Ms. Fairbearn, was married to him. Divorced now. I doubt they will think a Jaguar is related to a Grizzly Bear but you never know."

That brought on a round of laughs.

"There is a real Unicorn?"

"Oh Yes, he's quite unique and formidable. Right up your alley. I don't think he ever raced but he gives the Lion a run for his money every now and again. You have to meet them. They rent out this lounge. Fiona is their employee but their pub in the village is a real tourist attraction."

"I shall go. Perhaps David and Dan will want to come, too."

"I'm sure they will. I'll have Dougal arrange a trip for you."

We don't know how he does it but Dougal appeared at the mere mention of his name. As I mentioned, Dougal is a Shetland Sheep Dog, Estate Manager of Bearmoral Castle/Polar Paradise and Maître d' of the Hotel Dining Rooms.

"What ken I be doin' fer ye, Doctor Bear and Bearoness. It's glad I am to see the whole clan back again. Resort business is runnin' at a grand peak. Tons of tourists! Say, your Bairns have grown tremendous. Hello, Miz Chita! Mr. Maury! I haven't met this Gentlecat."

Belinda said, "Dougal, say hello to Señor Jaguar Jack the Lad. He is a good friend of ours. He would like to visit the Lion and Unicorn Pub before he goes back to Cincinnati day after tomorrow. I think he would like to take Lord David and Dancing Dan with him.

"Oh, aye. Happy to have a security and fire service at last. The tourists will love the fire truck, Flame."

"Well, the Cubs certainly do. BTW. When they hear there is to be an expedition to see the Lion and Unicorn, the Cubs will clamor to come along. It's OK."

"I'll be happy to lay on a jitney for all of ye tomorrer, Señor Jack! Would ten o'clock suit?"

"I should be recovered from my Tequila bout by then, Dougal. That would be fine. Can you invite David and Dan and the Cubs to join me?"

"That I can, Señor. Tomorrer at ten! Excuse me. I must dress for overseeing dinner."

Octavius leaned over to Jack "How is the horse race handicapping program going? That sounds like a good case for Deep Data analytics."

"Well, Señor Condor has put it back on the track. *(a snorting guffaw)* That self-important Cassowary had yanked my team for one of his projects."

"I think he was trying to use them in one of his extortion schemes. That's not going to happen. Caleb has flown the coop even if he is flightless."

"I am heading back to Kentucky to work out a test schedule. I think we have a winner on our hands. Would you care to come with me, Señorita Chita?

Chita slurped her champagne. "Maybe I'll join you, Jack. At the pub. Not back at the Hexagon. I haven't seen Lion in ages and Unicorn is a sketch. You'll love them. Fiona, my dear. How about a refill?"

Chita

Chapter Two

*(Narrator's Note: This Chapter is partially abstracted from Book 13
A Case of Déjà Vu.)*

*I guess now you have probably heard
Cassowary's a horrible bird.
He's a screwball and threat.
He's a real Space Cadet.
And his plans are quite clearly absurd.*

(Planet Gaea or possibly Biosphere X)

Caleb Cassowary is an avid avian supremacist. He believes that birds, directly descended as they are from the dinosaurs, have an historic right, priority and obligation to rule. To support his conviction, he has made an extensive study of the late, unconscionable Imperius Drake and has studiously endeavored to emulate his every move toward global domination.

Like his warped predecessor, Caleb harbors an extreme hatred for Octavius Bear and ursines in general. In fact, his animosity extends to most mammalian species. He is, after all, one of the world's most dangerous birds. Though he is flightless, his claws and kick can be fatal. Let's face it, he is a walking, feathered catastrophe. A most perilous character.

His former position as Chief Technical Officer of the Advanced Super Computing Center UUI, afforded him an outstanding opportunity to exercise his formidable genius in the pursuit of cosmic superiority by exploiting highly sophisticated technology. He had major plans to capitalize on it. They failed!

We believe his current, albeit temporary, exile on Gaea is the result of his assistant, Byzantia Bonobo meeting a chimp named Joel at an astrophysics conference. They had danced around the concept of Multiverse travel until he fessed up and admitted he was from a different world. He was an Adept and could transit between worlds at will.

She talked him into taking her with him on his next trip. It was then she discovered that she too was an Adept. She also discovered that Homo Sapiens still existed. There on Gaea! That was a real shock. Joel had used up his allotted "Earth Time" on the last trip and stayed on at Gaea. Byzz returned to Earth but thought seriously about permanent planetary emigration.

When she returned to Earth and the Hexagon, in a moment of weakness, she shared her secret with Caleb. It was a big mistake and unfortunately, irretrievable. He pressured her into accompanying her to Gaea. He was not an Adept – just a "Passive" – and required the services of an Adept or the use of a transmission device to make the journey.

In typical Caleb fashion, while on Gaea, he stole a small portable transit device and brought it back to Earth. It sat ready for his use in a nondescript alcove near the server farm on the third floor of the Hexagon. It would get lots of use with his designs for interplanetary conquest.

As might be expected, the former CTO was not content with traveling to one world. He was convinced there were many just waiting for him to conquer. He no longer needed Byzz to transit. He had the device and used it. Delusions of cosmic grandeur overcame his common sense and he began experimenting in earnest. His efforts often resulted in near disaster but he was not deterred.

Octavius Bear and that ridiculous Porcupine would no longer have a corner on Multiverse travel. As in all things technological and otherwise, they would have to contend with Caleb Cassowary. He set out to totally destroy the Bear's Empire through ransomware extortion. He botched it and brought international wrath down upon his wattled head. He and Byzz escaped, though.

He persists in his plans of cosmic domination. The galaxy will live in awe of him. No, not just one galaxy. His aspirations were intergalactic and beyond. In fact, as he considered it, his idol, Imperius Drake, was a piker. He only wanted world domination. Caleb looks far beyond that. The Multiverse! Gaea is just a start. He itched to kick out at Homo Sapiens. They once dominated the Earth and now Gaea. He will show them true dominance. He'll knock them into shape and then bury them with his startling intelligence. Then, with an army of interplanetary minions he will go on to conquer one sphere after another, including, of course, Earth.

He knew of Biosphere X – the bird exoplanet. They had sparred with the Octavians and suffered serious losses. Caleb would see that didn't happen again. Avians were superior and he, of course, is the supreme Avian.

CALEB CASSOWARY

The Development of Civilization Volume 14 Part 2
Aerospace Engineering

From "An Introduction to Faunapology"
by Octavius Bear Ph.D.

With our concentration on quantum motion in the Multiverse, it is easy to overlook our other activities in space. While hardly in the same league as NASA, SpaceX, Blue Origin, Virgin Galactic or Boeing, UUI Aerospace makes important contributions to rocket science and astrophysical experimentation.

Located on the Florida east coast, UUIA is a separate subsidiary dedicated to advancing Earth's missions in the Solar System and beyond. We work with a number of scientific and engineering organizations in developing platforms, instrumentation and propulsion systems for small and intermediate payloads to venture into the void.

All this is in addition to our somewhat secretive Multiverse endeavors which specialize in interplanetary travel for individuals. Quantum processes do not readily lend themselves to transporting devices, materials or vehicles through space. So we also engage in the rough and ready world of physical rocketry. We work with these other agencies to place our own satellites in orbit and conduct communications tests and exploration.

Avoiding asteroids and space junk is another significant undertaking. Space navigation techniques are part of the Advanced Super Computing Center's mission and are assigned to a special group of high powered mathematicians and physicists. They were not affected by the recent Cassowary inspired disruptions.

UUIA contracts with a range of private and governmental entities worldwide but is also engaged in a series of highly secretive tasks for US Intelligence and Defense agencies.

I am personally privileged to have access to this work but I cannot share my knowledge beyond the security limits imposed by the government. Suffice it to say that we keep it completely separated from our other computational and communications activities.

Chapter Three

The team is now meeting on Zoom.
There's a definite feeling of gloom.
They all feel insecure
And Belinda is sure
That wretch Caleb is plotting their doom.

Belinda was worried. With that hate crazed Cassowary on the loose, no one was safe. It was clear he loathed Octavius and was only too eager to bring about death and destruction to the world at large in order to establish his supremacy. She was fearful for her husband, the Cubs, the Octavians and for that matter, all of civilization. Were UUI, the Hexagon, the Bear's Lair and Polar Paradise still safe?

"Tavi, what are we doing to rein Caleb in?"

"Plenty, Bel. We think we have tracked him down. Global law enforcement and the military are involved. He is either on Gaea or Biosphere X."

"Biosphere X? That's the Home World of those insanely belligerent birds. They tried to fire bomb UUI and the Lair. They're worse than Caleb. What an awful combination!"

"General Turmoil's attack on them in retribution for their assaults here has toned them down a good deal. He killed off the Protector *(Their Leader)* and the entire governing Council. He did quite a bit of physical damage in the process. They'll think twice before staging another attack."

"But they must be boiling over with thoughts of revenge. Caleb is just the screwball to feed that rage. Sorry, I don't share your confidence."

"I'm not confident. I want him stopped even more than you do. We have an action plan and we're about to implement it."

"If I can help, just ask."

"We'll be activating everyone. *(Well almost everyone. Keep the Cubs in check.)* Hold tight!"

*****

Behold! The Advanced Super Computing Center of UUI. Until recently the exclusive domain of Caleb Cassowary, who is now on the run in Quantum Space. Senhor L. Condor, *(Condo)* Brazilian communications and computing virtuoso has taken charge at Octavius' behest. It is an impressive place and he is an impressive genius. Another bird but vastly different from crazy Caleb.

Envision a mile-square, four story, six sided, copper colored structure capped with antennas, a helipad and solar panel arrays and surrounded by wind turbines and parking lots. The bottom two stories are taken up with utilities and power supplies feeding the insatiable demands of the main frames, servers and quantum computing units that completely occupy the third floor. The top floor is mostly open plan with work and gathering spaces where designers, developers, programmers, coders, data analysts, cloud and artificial intelligence support teams ply their respective trades. The Pentagon on steroids. Tucked away in one wing is a column of offices assigned to the Hex management brain trust. Condo has taken over Caleb's offices.

He is sitting in front of a large screen in a Zoom session with Howard Watt, Marlin, Octavius, Colonel Wyatt Where and me. Ursula 12 occupies one panel of the display.

As usual, Octavius has taken the lead. "Greetings, all. Time for a brief status report. Settling in, Condo?"

"Getting there, Octavius. This place can be overwhelming. The staff is superb. I will say this for Caleb. He selected highly talented people."

I laughed, "But then ran roughshod over all of them."

"True, Maury, hatred of him was practically universal but most of them stayed on because they were immersed in spectacular projects with a pack of geniuses. Of course, Octavius, you've been paying them very well."

"It helps. Are you convinced of their loyalties to the Center and UUI? We still have quite a mess to clean up and the business demands are accelerating in spite of the recent wreckage by Caleb."

"I'd be lying if I said my confidence level is at a peak but we're coping nicely. The satellites are back online. The Cloud is flourishing. Deep Data analysis is on the rise. The press has found other things to occupy their attention and most regulators have calmed down. Wolford and the other legal eagles have a lot on their plate. Piles of lawsuits."

"There are also several mergers and acquisitions waiting in the wings. I gather these suitors and suitees feel a lot more comfortable with us now that the Cassowary has departed. Do we have any idea where he is?"

Howard cut in. "The odds are heavily in favor of him hiding out on Gaea. We're still shaking down our tracking systems. Marlin has been fine tuning the design and if Caleb makes a move, we think we can tag him."

The Dolphin splashed affirmation. "He's not going to lay low for long. He's on a mission and his ego can't grasp the idea of defeat. He's a master at self-delusion. He'll be making moves shortly. He's compulsive. We still don't know what to make of his assistant, though. Any thoughts, Ursula?"

As usual, the AGI was taking all this in, analyzing and measuring as she went. "Byzz and I have a history. Truth be told, she is my primary designer although as he always did, Caleb took all of the credit for developing the Ursulas. *(It's a separate subject but we need to make some decisions about the creation of Ursula 13. I am hardly obsolete but the line could use some upgrades.)*"

"My opinion is that Byzz is stuck. She never wanted to be part of Caleb's nutty scheme but now she finds herself a fugitive facing at a minimum, charges of aiding and abetting. She can't return to Earth although I'm not sure she wants to. I think she just wants to escape from that Cassowary."

"It's possible Caleb will cast her off. He will surround himself with a corps of toadies ready to cater to his limitless ego as he proceeds with his dreams of conquest. In his narcissistic mind, she's probably excess baggage. She's a Multiverse Adept and he's a Passive but he has that quantum device he's stolen so he doesn't need her to travel the galaxies. On the other hand, if she gets her act together, she can strike out on her own. She's a certified genius and a technical whiz. I'm sorry we lost her. The Ursula program is poorer as a result."

"We need to also bear in mind that Caleb is currently running around with an immense amount of Top-Secret and Beyond material in that grotesque head of his. I don't know what clearances Byzz had."

This produced a few moments of silence from the other Zoom participants.

Condo reacted first. "We must track him down. You should also know developing Ursula 13 is high on my priority list. I intend to rapidly appoint a replacement for Byzantia either from the Hexagon staff or an outsider. Suggestions are more than welcome."

The Colonel commented. "Change of subject. There are crowds of law enforcement representatives eager to get their paws on Caleb. Charges, subpoenas and indictments are tumbling all over. Several states, countries and international organizations want to invoke extradition proceedings. He's charged with multiple counts of extortion; willful destruction of property; interruption of commerce; national security breaches; attempted violence against individuals and a host of other violations and infringements. He may even have caused a few deaths. The law types went berserk when he and his assistant escaped from the Hexagon."

"Most of the coppers believe he is hiding out somewhere here on Earth. Few of them have any understanding or belief in the Multiverse. Gaea or any of the other populated exoplanets just don't exist. One exception is FBI Special Agent Honey Badger. She's had experience with us before and knows that alternate worlds are out there. She also knows about the Ursulas. Chief Inspector Wallaroo and I are both working with her."

I raised a paw. "You said a magic word, Wyatt. Bruce Wallaroo. Where is he?"

Octavius replied. "On his way here. Interpol reassigned him to work on this case. He'll be flying in shortly. The Cubs will be elated. So will I."

Ursula chimed in *(literally)* "You know, we should have included Otto and the Frau in this session. They have major contributions to make. Otto has become our premiere quantum traveler and the Frau doesn't have her domestic issues to worry about while she's here at the castle. She can be a great help. By the way, Doctor Bear, how is the new Butler working out at the Lair?"

"Huntley? He seems to be adapting very nicely. Belinda and the Frau are both pleased. They've been turning over more and more assignments to him. I like him. The Cubs like him. They want him in their game along with the rest of the world. What do you think, Maury?"

I was still fence sitting. "So far, so good!"

Howard and Marlin approved of him. Condo had moved out of the mansion and taken rooms near the Hexagon so he had no opinion. The Colonel was noticeably quiet. A handsome Husky around the Frau may not have been sitting all that well with him. A little jealousy perhaps? We shall see.

The Bear turned to Howard. "Is it time for a little Gaean reconnaissance? What's your confidence level that he's there?"

"Pretty high but we can't be sure until we actually spot him. He could be on Biosphere X with those nutty birds or elsewhere. He'll certainly stick out. How many Cassowarys do you think are on those planets?"

"Next to none. He knows who you are, Howard and Wyatt, and he can't stand you, Maury. Sounds like another spy job for Otto. He loves this stuff. See if you can get him up on the screen."

The Zoom screen shifted and a goofy face came up in a new panel. Otto was staring into his laptop. "You rang?"

"Yes, your Magnificence. We have need of your wonderful skills."

"I live to serve. What ridiculous assignment have you prepared for me this time, Maury?"

"We want you to find Caleb. We don't think he knows you."

"Dead or alive?"

"You or him?"

"Him!"

"Alive is preferable but dead will be acceptable."

"Where is he supposed to be. Just give me a hint."

"Gaea! Or Possibly Biosphere X"

"Ah, Gaea or Biosphere X. Many an evening I have spent being chased around crumby planets. Hey, Meerkat! Just once can I go someplace nice?"

"Next time. I promise. Howard and Marlin have the specs for this trip. Bring an Ursula with you, of course."

"Of course! Gaea's a big place. What do I do when I get there?"

"Nose around. Establish contacts. He's unique. Someone will know him. He's probably already making enemies for himself. Somebody will want to get at him. He'll probably antagonize all the Homo Sapiens with his avian superiority crap. Track him down but don't try to capture him. Have Ursula call us. We'll come and support you. Remember, he can be a killer with those legs."

"I still have bruises from that crazy Zebra on Rhea. I can roll with a punch."

"But how about a kick with massive claws?"

Octavius interrupted, "He may have taken off for Biosphere X or someplace else. He has a portable quantum travel device. Howard, we should have grabbed that back at the Hexagon. Otto, see if you can find Byzz. She'll probably seek technical work. Very possibly with small satellites. Those and the Ursulas are her specialties. We're going to send you to the Gaea Telecommunications and Computing Center. Be your inconspicuous self."

"I am the soul of inconspicuosity – is that a word?

"No!"

Chapter Four

Now Caleb was clearly absurd.
No, 'deadly" is really the word.
But Condo instead
Just keeps plugging ahead.
He's quite a remarkable bird.

Let us briefly return to The Advanced Super Computing Center of UUI - the Hexagon - and consider once again Senhor L. Condor, *(Condo)* newly appointed CTO of the complex.

Condo is an Andean Condor with a twelve foot wingspan, *Vultur Gryphus,* a native of the South American wilds. He came in from the mountains and established himself in Sao Paolo, one of the world's largest cities, to pursue his passion for telecommunications. It started out as compensation for the fact that Andean Condors have no voice box and can't make any kind of vocal sound. *(See Book 2 – The Case of the Spotted Band.)* The Condor has since remedied that through the wonders of microchip technology and avian biology. Today, courtesy of a highly miniaturized, embedded vocal device, he can create any sound and often entertains by imitating the voices of his audience.

Bruce Wallaroo has known Condo for quite a while. I first met him when Bruce and I were on the run from a Brazilian gangster named Pontius Puma. Condo used his impressive network equipment and phenomenal technical knowledge to totally destroy the Puma's criminal infrastructure.

We exited Sao Paolo with three of the four members of the Spotted Band who were also on Pontius Puma's hit list. Chita was the fourth member but had taken off separately. This was before she joined the good guys and ended up as a card carrying Octavian.

Belinda took the Aquabear SST to Sao Paolo on a rescue mission and after some neat work finessing customs and border police flew the six of us back to Cincinnati.

With the Puma seeking revenge, the Condor decided things were too hot for him in Brazil and since he had shut down his personal tech center before leaving, he decided to stay a while with us at the Bear's Lair.

A while became a long while and Condo has settled in with us and has participated in a number of wild adventures that I have recorded in the many volumes of the Casebooks. He has become an active and essential Octavian.

As I said, he is a technical genius. Certainly on a par and probably more advanced than Caleb Cassowary. When that dirty bird staged his extortion try and failed, he and his assistant Byzz headed for the hills. That is, another planet courtesy of the wonders of Multiverse travel. That left a gap at the top of the Hexagon and Octavius called on Condo to fill it.

He is doing exceptionally well in command of the Advanced Center.

It didn't take very long for the Center staff to rally around him and after picking up the pieces caused by Caleb's blitz, they have UUI's global telecom and computing offerings on an even keel and advancing admirably. The Cloud and Deep Data Analytics businesses are going gangbusters.

A piece of the puzzle still not firmly in place is the Ursula advancement program. These robotic marvels have served us brilliantly to the point that we cannot function without them. The program was under the direction of Byzz. Caleb was far too busy in his own mind to devote any of his precious talent to the project. Conquest is his number one objective.

At the moment, Ursula 12 is filling in as Condo's assistant and aiding in the development of Ursula 13. This is in addition to her ubiquitous support throughout the Octavian universe.

You will be hearing much more about Condo and his fantastic, if only temporary, assistant as our story progresses. Stand by.

Meanwhile…

Chapter Five

Mother Russia's most fabulous son
Has returned for another first run.
He'll swashbuckle his way
And then end up the day
With another "fine film full of fun"

Yet another shuttle helicopter settled onto the Bearmoral helipad bringing more guests to the hotel. This time however, the passengers were not the first time tourist bears staring excitedly at the huge pile overlooking the North Sea. The rotors spun down to a halt and seven animals descended from the fuselage. They stood by as the staff porters retrieved their luggage.

Chita and I had been curiously examining Flame, the fire engine, inspecting her elaborate equipment. The Cat looked over at the whirlybird and said, "Hey Mr. Talent Agent. Guess who's here."

I was thunderstruck or at least mildly surprised. There standing next to the chopper's skids was the famous Russian star of the silver screen, TV, computer and smart phone. Preston Pavel Polar. The stellar Bear waved.

Chita gave me a questioning look. "Were you expecting him?

"Nope. I had no idea he was coming." I got on my cell phone and called Octavius. "Hold on to your vodka. Preston Polar and a small entourage just arrived."

"Did you invite him?"

"Not me. Check with Dougal. Does Belinda know?"

Conversation in the background. "She didn't know and Dougal says he didn't tell us because he thought we had invited them. They have reserved rooms."

By this time, the group had directed the porters to bring their luggage and array of equipment inside and Preston came over to me.

"Maury, my 'друг'! Hello again. We are here."

"'Good to see you again, Preston. What brings you back to Polar Paradise?"

"Why, another film, of course. Didn't you get my message?"

"Sorry, no!"

He turned to his two Grizzly Bear production assistants. "Doris, Ella, did you send the message?"

Each one shook their heads and then waited for the blast in Russian.

I intervened. "Never mind. We're happy to see you and I'm sure we have rooms for you. Herr Schäferhund, happy to see you again."

The German Shepherd producer extended a paw in greeting.

"Sheldon and Seymour Raccoon. Scriptwriters and Scenarists extraordinaire! How are you?"

"As well as can be expected. We hate helicopters."

I looked at Preston. "Still no agent, I see. Going it alone?"

"My lawyer, Sasha Sable, will be coming up later."

"And who is this young lady?" I looked at a youthful and highly attractive polar sow. No doubt, Preston's latest ingenue squeeze. His last companion ended up taking a plunge into the sea from a balcony here at the hotel. I hope this one had better luck.

Preston said, "Bree, say hello to Maury Meerkat, an excellent talent agent. You'll want to get acquainted."

"Hello, Mr. Meerkat." she simpered.

"Oh Boy!" I turned to him. "Another film, Preston? More derring-do?"

"Of course! What is this fire engine?"

"This is Flame. She's a very unusual fire truck."

"Gustav, Seymour, Sheldon, we have to use this truck!"

The producer winced but then nodded his head, the writers shrugged. Another Preston Pavel Polar whim.. Ah well!

I said, "Come into the hotel. I'm sure Octavius and Belinda will be delighted to see you all again. *(I can lie with a straight face although Bel really enjoyed her stints in front of the cameras. The Cubs will be delighted. Octavius not so much.)* We have several new guests you'll want to meet."

Chita strolled over and was promptly kissed by the great Romancer. "Ms. Chita, what a pleasure to see you again. Your act as a gangster's moll has created a sensation. You must do it again."

Bree was frowning. "Was this cat competition?"

We reached the lobby and strolled into the salon. The tourists were all atwitter. "Isn't that the famous Polar Bear screen star?"

"Yes, it is. Oh, this is so exciting." Spontaneous Applause!

Preston, ever sensitive to his audiences, twirled into one of his many swashbuckling poses, spread his paws, laughed and then bowed. More applause.

The Octavians were seated in a corner of the lounge taking all this in. Chita walked back and joined them while I skittered up to Bel and Octavius, "The Russians have invaded." *(Actually, Preston was the only Russian. Not sure where Bree came from.)*

Belinda rose and pecked the star on the cheek. "Preston Pavel Polar, Back again! How good to see you."

"And you, Bearoness. You are looking your fabulous self. Hello, Doctor Bear. You are looking well too, in spite of your recent catastrophe."

Octavius snorted. "Oh, you know about that."

"Oh yes. All of the digital copies of our films are out on your Cloud. It was a near disaster. I'm delighted it's been restored. We are now using two Cloud services. I hope you understand."

The Great Bear understood, all right. Many of our clients were doing the same thing. Caleb had caused some serious damage.

"Have you caught up with the perpetrator."

"Not yet. He escaped and is evading us but we'll nab him." *(The Bear did not mention that we believed he was on another world. We don't think*

Preston knows about Multiverse travel and we were not about to enlighten him.) But come. Let's get some introductions under way. You haven't met a few of these animals."

He made the rounds of the group. Lord David got special attention. Preston had fallen in love with Flame and wanted to use her. In fact, he wanted to buy her. Flame was not for sale and Uncle Davey seemed a bit dubious about letting the truck appear in the film. Dan talked him into it. Jack mentioned that they were going to see Lion and Unicorn in situ tomorrow and invited Herr Schäferhund to join the merry band. "Maybe they could be in your next epic."

Gustav was delighted. Bree was already gob smacked by this wild assortment of beings but was not prepared for the next edition. The Cubs!! Into the lounge tumbled the Furballs. "Uncle Preston. Hi! Are you making another picture? Can we be in it? We're running a new Internet game. The Bold Brave Brilliant Bumptious Bears. We have over a million subscribers. Would you like to be one of our characters? We have a bunch of royalty but no movie star. Are you going to be the dashing swordsbear again?"

Preston laughed. "No, my young friends. This time Preston Pavel Polar will fight in the 21st century." He looked at Octavius and Bel. "I have decided, based on your recent attacks to make a film about combatting Cyber Terrorists. Very high tech. I may use a light saber. This castle will be my headquarters. Bree will be my assistant. She gets captured. *(This was news to Bree.)* The evil terrorist will operate from a site like your Hexagon. I rescue her and defeat the Cyber Villain. All this with your agreement, of course."

Belinda and Chita seemed fascinated. Octavius was reticent. The Cubs jumped with excitement. The Frau, Colonel and Mlle Woof were dubious.

He continued, "I need to find an appropriate villain. I understand your opponent was *(is)* a Southern Cassowary. They certainly look evil. Where can we find one?"

Bruce Wallaroo who had been silent *(surprise)* while all this was going on, intervened. "They're all over Australia, mate. Send one of your assistants down to Sydney or Melbourne. You should be able to find enough to staff twenty epics. They'll be glad of the work."

"Thank you Inspector. Would you like to be a technical advisor?"

"I'll have to ask Interpol."

Chapter Six

Should a meerkat voyage out on the sea?
That just doesn't seem prudent to me!
But what can you do
When the Bear says to you:
"Get a move on! You're sailing with me!"

(On the Way to see the Prince of Whales)

Octavius finished off up his hearty Scottish breakfast, rose, looked over at Otto and me and asked, "Ready for a boat ride? Fetch the Cubs."

I had almost forgotten our planned trip into the mists of the North Sea. And the Cubs were coming. This would be interesting. I called for Mlle Woof and asked her to bring the Furballs down. When she heard we were going out on the sea in a boat she begged off accompanying us. Like Chita, she hated water. She wasn't crazy about the Cubs making the trip, either.

As usual, the Furballs were beside themselves with excitement. "Where are we going, Poppa? Can we sail the boat? Are we going to catch some fish?"

Otto shook his head and said, "I'll check and make sure Harold is ready."

Harold is a sea otter in charge of all things aquatic at Polar Paradise. He would be piloting the sizeable craft. Sizing up Octavius, Otto said, "I guess we'd better use the big whaler." He 'zapped' off.

Octavius guffawed, leaving all of us wondering what was going on in that ursine head. Smiling, *(an infrequent occurrence)* he led us out of the dining room, through the hallways, over the moat, down to the beach and out on the floating dock where Harold and Otto were waiting with the 50 foot whaler at the ready. It took the three of us plus a lot of flailing and near capsizing to get Octavius into the boat. The capering Cubs didn't help much. I thought Otto might have tried to use his telekinetic powers but I think he was afraid to try them out on the Great Bear. After rolling about on the deck several times, Octavius finally righted himself and asked Harold, "How far is it to the seriously deep water?"

Another puzzle! Although I remembered a similar trip a few years ago.

Harold looked out to the east and said. "The shelf under the North Sea falls off pretty sharply about three miles out. There are some places so deep, they've never been measured."

"Excellent!" shouted the Bear. "That's exactly what I want!"

I hadn't noticed till then that he had been toting a very large sea bag. He trundled over to it and began to lift out a mass of electrical cables, his oversized laptop and several yellow boxes that looked like they were water sealed. Spreading the cables, he began to hook them up to the laptop and to the boxes.

"Might I enquire as to what you are doing? Are we going to trawl for undersea wildlife? We're not visiting royalty again, are we?"

He looked up from his sorting and plugging, grinned and said, "Astute of you. In a manner of speaking, yes! I realize I am asking a lot of you, Maury, and of both of you otters but just be patient until Harold gets us to the briny deep. And keep the Cubs from falling overboard. McTavish is trying to climb the mainmast."

Otto and I knew better than to try to pry open the Octavius Cone of Silence and Harold was too busy navigating and steering to have much time for questions. Thus it went for about an hour. Bouncing on a mildly choppy sea and becoming reacquainted with my breakfast several times, that barf bag attachment for my tail made more and more sense. I'll have to look into it.

Octavius went on plugging and unplugging, testing and re-testing. Among his instruments, I recognized an oversized UUI PeaPod universal language translator. This model was called the SeaPod. Otto, oblivious to all of the Bear's mysterious machinations had tossed himself off the boat several times and rode on the bow wave and then bobbed around in our wake. To Octavius' annoyance, Harold had to stop once or twice to pick him up.

"Otto, stay on board. You never know who's swimming around out here! You're holding us up."

Finally, Harold looked up from the helm, craned his head over the bathometer and said, "It's over three miles deep here, Mr. Bear!"

"Wonderful, Harold, slow down and then keep station and you two help me set up this gear."

"What you are about to toss over the side, Otto, is a high powered sound emitter along with a hydrophone for picking up undersea noises. They are both connected to my laptop which is programmed to create and send out very loud echolocation clicks to summon sperm whales. That in turn is connected to a conference size UUI Sea Pod universal translator."

Now, I slept through most of my school classes on Zoology and Faunapology but I did know that sperm whales are just about the largest living mammals on earth, second only to their blue cousins.

"You are planning to call up a sperm whale?"

"Not just any whale, Maury. The Prince of Whales! You no doubt saw his portrait hanging in the Lion and Unicorn. You met him on our last trip out."

"Yeah and from what I remember, he is big. A lot bigger than you - which is saying quite a lot." Octavius usually is the biggest beast among the various crowds we run in. An occasional hippo, giraffe or rhinoceros might come in with more weight, height or mass but generally, The Great Bear is The GREAT Bear.

"Yes," said the Bear, adopting his most professorial tone. "The sperm whale is the largest toothed whale, with adult males measuring up to 67 feet long and weighing up to 63 tons. They also have the largest brain of any known animal on earth. The blue whale is somewhat larger but they have no teeth and their brains are relatively smaller. The Prince of Whales, as you might expect, exceeds these proportions. Nobody has actually measured him but from our previous meetings, I would estimate he is close to 75 feet long and weighs at least 80 tons."

"Previous meetings? I remember only one."

"But several for me, in fact. As you have already seen, the logistics involved in settling down for an afternoon chat with him can be rather formidable. By the way, all of you, do NOT refer to this boat as a whaler while he is present. It's a touchy subject. He is true royalty but not in the least condescending or abrupt. In fact, he is quite charming, highly intelligent, an excellent thinker and commentator and I'm sure, quite attractive to the female members of his species."

Otto gulped, "And just like that, we're going to summon him up from the deep. How do you even know he is here?"

"Yesterday, I chatted with several dolphins who are part of his entourage. They said he winters here in the North Sea. With this echolocation gear, I will send out a message of clicks requesting an audience. The sound is quite loud and can be heard for hundreds of miles. Otto and Harold, don't get too close to the loudspeaker if you're in the water and of course, be very careful of approaching him at close range. By the way, don't speak to him until he has spoken first."

"I wouldn't think of it, Octavius. I'm careful about approaching or speaking to you."

The bear laughed, a substantial noise in itself. Harold stood at the helm, wondering how fast he could get the boat out of the vicinity if Octavius' scheme didn't quite work out. Of course, he mentioned nothing of this to the bear. A 9 foot bear or a 75 foot whale! After a certain point, size no longer matters to a 3 foot otter. With the bear, you could run but you can't hide and with the whale you can swim…but not for long.

"Alright," said Octavius, "let's get this rig over the side and the show on the road." *(This in the middle of a sea that is over three miles deep. Similes and metaphors are not Octavius' strong suit.)*

Firmly anchoring the laptop and language converter on the deck we paid out the cables attached to the underwater speakers and the hydrophone. When they had reached their limit, Octavius hit a key on the computer and a rush of bubbles and waves erupted next to the boat. We were "clicking." Sperm whale "clicking" is used by them for communication, hunting, and navigation – sort of a combined sonar and undersea conversation medium coupled with a fast food ordering system. Many whales sing. I found out that sperms don't. They click. Their voice and hearing apparatus is contained in their jaws and the sounds they produce are nerve-rackingly loud. More like "booms" than "clicks."

Otto's tours of duty in the Nevada casinos came to the surface. *(pun intended)* "What are the odds of us reaching him and of him coming to us, Octavius?"

"Wait and see, Otto!" Octavius was being his inscrutable self. I wondered if two otters and a meerkat could push him over the side. Maybe Otto could teleport him over. Nah, there'd be repercussions. So we sat and waited and waited and waited. The language converter repeated the clicks we were transmitting.

Needless to say, the Cubs were short on patience. "Why are we sitting here, Poppa? Aren't we going to catch some fish? Uncle Maury, what was all that stuff you threw over the side. What's that clicking noise?"

"Doctor Bear," said Harold, "What are you saying to him?"

"Just reminding him of our last meeting and inviting him up for a chin wag. Granted, he has quite a chin to wag."

Suddenly a small school of dolphins broke the water and swam around the boat, fascinating the Cubs. One, no doubt the spokesman of the group, started chattering at Octavius. The bear raised his paws, signaling "wait a minute," turned to the Sea Pod and computer, flipped a few switches, turned back to the dolphin and said, "Go ahead" in dolphin squeak. The bottle nose braced his flippers along the side of the boat while the others circled behind him.

"His Highness asked us to tell you he is feeding at the moment but will be along shortly. He says he remembers you. He doesn't know very many bears *(live ones, that is.)*

"Please tell His Royal Highness that I await his pleasure and look forward to renewing our acquaintance."

The dolphin nodded his head and blew out a spray from his nose that splattered on the deck *(not sure whether that was meaningful, playful or just getting ready for a long dive.)* He turned, seemingly rotating on his tail, leapt into a ring formed by his fellows and disappeared. Octavius reset the systems to whale conversation.

I couldn't resist. "This guy really does the royalty thing up brown, doesn't he?"

"Well," said the Bear, "Remember where you are. Monarchies are an integral part of the UK character. His father, the King, is reaching his 85th birthday and has turned over most of the royal privileges and duties to his son who I estimate to be about thirty. Whales can be very long-lived. Because he has now taken on the mantle of sovereignty, I expected he would be staying closer to home here in the North Sea. When I first met him, he was something of a play whale, travelling the world, attending all sorts of events and no doubt chasing his share of females. I know he has grown more serious, now."

"Excuse me, Octavius, this is all very interesting and I look forward to meeting the Royal Whale yet again but why are we here? I can't imagine you are simply socializing in the middle of all the mess we're in."

"Absolutely not, Otto, this is hardly a social call. Just be patient!"

Suddenly a geyser of air and water blasted out of the sea. It was close enough to drench us as we stood on the deck of the boat. The Cubs ran for cover and then returned, gaping in amazement. They were mesmerized.

A squared off mountain of dark grey skin raised itself slowly above the waves, followed by the largest jaw it has ever been my fortune *(good or otherwise)* to see. A relatively small eye set back and above the jaw and just forward of a flipper stared at us intently. I looked up and saw a dorsal fin emerge near the stern of the boat and much further out a gigantic fluke smacked the surface of the water. Yes, this was a big animal. A very big animal. Once again, I was awed. I tried only semi-successfully to keep my knees from knocking. I looked at Harold and Otto. Their jaws were at full drop.

The whale clicked loudly and the translator roared, "Your pardon for the drenching. I sneezed. I think I'm getting allergic to squid. Ah, yes, now that I see you I remember you quite well, Doctor Bear. Welcome back to the North Sea of which I am Prince Regent."

Octavius bowed his head just a bit and replied, "Thank you, Your Highness. I am privileged and delighted to see you again. May I present my associates, first: Our pilot is Mr. Harold Otter who is in the employ of Bearoness Belinda Bruin at Bearmoral Castle."

"Ah, yes The Bearoness. Never met her snout to snout but I have heard much about her, all quite favorable. Pity about her husband's accident. Do you think she'll ever re-mate?"

Octavius is usually as smooth as they come in one on one conversation. *(He only disappoints when he is making a formal speech.)* All three of us were watching his face and listening to what he might say.

"I think it is in the realm of possibility, sir. She is a most attractive sow."

"Well, let's hope some lucky polar sweeps her off her paws. Not good to have the nobility, even dubious nobility, *(the eye winked)* without issue to continue the line."

"I have mated since we last met, your Highness. Let me introduce my two cubs, Arabella and McTavish'

"Hello, young ones. What strange but attractive coloration they have, Doctor Bear."

"Poppa, why don't you tell him who Momma is?"

This time Octavius sneezed or unleashed something closely approximating one. He looked at the Cubs and raised his eyebrows. They got the message. "Shut up!"

The Prince chortled *(setting off a sonic boom)* "God bless you, Doctor Bear! There must be something going around. I hope you're not allergic to whales. And who are these two worthies?"

He'd forgotten. I guess he ran into too many commoners to have us all in his memory.

The Great Bear recovered and pointing to me, said, "Your Highness, may I re-introduce Mr. Mauritius Meerkat, formerly of South Africa and the isle of Mauritius, now an American. He is my trusted assistant and confidant."

The whale squinted at me and said, "I don't think I have ever met a meerkat before, Mr. Mauritius. In what way are you related to the feline species?"

Yes, he'd forgotten. Oh boy, here we go again. The Unicorn Conversation! "I am not a feline, Your Highness. The name is an unfortunate misstatement brought about by some Dutch naturalist who was visiting Africa. I think he was a near-sighted mole." I almost launched off into my relationship to a mongoose but decided that once around that track was enough for one trip to Scotland.

Octavius interposed. "Finally, this young otter, a North American River Otter, is an associate of Mr. Meerkat and myself. His name is Hairy Otter but he is popularly known as Otto the Magnificent, a stage name. He is a performer with a few rather remarkable abilities. How he got them we need not discuss. I'm not sure how much longer you wish to stay on the surface, sir, but it does bring me to my reason for seeking an audience."

"I may sound once or twice during our visit but I shall return immediately. By the way, I think we can dispense with the royal formalities. *(I thought I heard a squeak from one of the dolphins who had been swimming close by.)* That was my equerry, Sir Flipsalot. He's a stickler for the proprieties. I am not. Please call me Bertie and I shall call you what I believe I called you in Alaska – Tavi. And gentlebeasts, will Harold, Mauritius and Otto do?"

"Please call me Maury….er Bertie!"

The whale laughed again, almost swamping the boat. "Now what has occasioned your visit, Tavi? Have you come to beg a boon? (Another chortle!)

"In a manner of speaking, yes, Bertie. You may recall lending us the Dolphin Marlin, your Chief Scientist, Magician and part time Jester. Our agreed upon time for his services is up and I was hoping to extend his stay with us. He has been exceptionally valuable in a number of our programs.

"Marlin! Yes, I remember now. I wondered what happened to him. You had him. Excuse me! I feel the urge to sound. I shall return shortly."

With a resounding smack from his fluke and a rush of water surrounding his submerging body, the Whale dove straight down into the 3 mile depth leaving us and a few of his dolphin "court" to await his return. His departure had rocked the whale boat dramatically and for a moment it looked like we were going to have to call upon the dolphins to help stabilize the craft. We switched the translator to its "dolphin" setting and looked out at the cavorting bottle nose Flipsalot who had first approached us before the Prince's arrival.

"How deep does he go when he does that?" I asked.

"It depends," came the squeaky return. "He'll probably only go a few thousand fathoms before coming up again. I don't think he took in as much air as he might have wanted to."

"By the way, all of us could understand the click exchange between His Highness and yourselves so we are aware of your request. That SeaPod translator device of yours developed by Marlin is quite competent. It works beautifully for undersea life. Thank you!"

Before I could get into the discussion, the Prince had resurfaced, surrounded by several members of his retinue including the ever present equerry, Sir Flipsalot. His entrances and departures were, not to put too fine a point on it, dramatic and aquatic. Water, water everywhere, mostly on our deck and all over me. Octavius was dampened, the otters didn't care but I almost drowned. Being small may have its advantages but not in this case. The Cubs were soaked and none too happy about it. Still, they looked on in amazement.

"That was a shorter dive than I intended but I did want to get back to our discussion," boomed the whale. "While below, I remembered our agreement about Marlin. I also am very grateful for the translation devices you have given us. I understand Marlin was the designer.'

"Bertie, you are welcome. Marlin is a godsend. May we hold onto him? I know he wants to stay with us. Right now, he is assisting us in fighting off a very serious threat by a psychotic bird and his followers. *(Not exactly true but close enough!)*"

"Well, as a sovereign-to-be and current Regent, I cannot ignore any phenomenon that may threaten or enhance the lives of my subjects. You and I must open a clear information channel."

"Indeed, sir, and as one step in that direction, I believe Marlin will be a great assist."

Thankfully, the Prince was in a good mood. "I guess by letting Marlin join you, temporarily, mind, I have expanded my own contacts and information sources. Alright, Marlin may stay with you."

Spontaneously, Otto rejoiced and flipped from the deck in a series of somersaults. He swam around in circles and then to the amazement of the Prince and his courtiers, zapped back onto the deck.

"Does he do that often?" asked the Prince.

"Often enough, Your Highness! *(back to formality as we were taking our leave)* We will leave the details of mutual communication to Marlin to arrange. We in turn, will communicate with him through my aide, Maury and our friendly otter, Otto the Magnificent. *(I bowed and Otto blushed.)* We expect to be here in Scotland for at least another week. But we have several ongoing projects at Bearmoral that will require return visits, so I shall be shuttling back and forth in the future. I thank you for your assistance. It was delightful to see you again." *(slight bow)*

"I enjoyed it, Doctor Bear and I am looking forward to continuing a fruitful relationship. Tell Marlin he is still a member of the court and to deport himself appropriately. Remember he started out as my Court Jester."

We remembered. When Marlin is at Polar Paradise, he often joins Otto in his hijinks with the Aquabears.

The Prince clicked, "You there, Helm! Perhaps you should move your boat off a ways before I break for the depths. I gather I create quite a splash." He looked at sodden me and winked.

Chapter Seven

We returned with our whale of a tale
About seeing His Highness the Whale.
Meeting royalty's great!
But I'm forced to relate
I got soaked from my head to my tail.

(Back at Bearmoral)

When we came back from our whaling expedition, we rounded up Belinda, the Colonel and Frau Schuylkill, called Howard and Marlin and roused the other Octavians. Octavius wanted to tell his story After all, commoners didn't just show up at the Prince's watery doorstep every day. On the other hand, Octavius Bear wasn't just another commoner.

We started to tell them about our meeting with the Prince of Whales. Belinda seemed a bit annoyed at being left out until Octavius said, "Since you are a member of the nobility, we weren't sure, if we would have to go through all sorts of formalities. This way, we unsophisticated Americans *(Harold excepted)* could just plead bad manners if there was any kind of a flap. Besides, I knew him from previous visits. Remember the shifting oil rigs? Anyway, He does send you his kindest regards."

This seemed to mollify the Bearoness. Needless to say the Frau, a great respecter of crowned heads, nobility and aristocracy was impressed all to hell with our gaining a royal audience so easily.

Marlin and Howard were delighted that Prince Bertie had agreed to letting him stay on. They had a number of Multiverse projects to continue. Octavius had not mentioned Multiverse to the Prince. He measured his world in fathoms. He was a noble, if somewhat forgetful soul.

The Cubs were beside themselves in excitement. The inevitable surfaced. *(No Pun!!)*

"Poppa and Momma, we need to get the Prince of Whales and his dolphins into our game. The Bold Brave Brilliant Bumptious Bears and the Royal Court. A duke, a duchess, a Chamberlain and now a Prince. Wow!

The Development of Civilization Volume 14 Part 3
Small Satellites
From "An Introduction to Faunapology"
by Octavius Bear Ph.D.

Satellite TV and GPS are commonplace systems that we now take for granted. Asked to describe them, the average citizen will outline the services and their various functions. When pressed further some will conjure up images of large, winged devices locked in stationary orbit around the world's circumference, beaming down immense streams of data to upraised antennas and leave it at that. All true but it is only an incomplete picture of the satellite panoply that occupies our atmosphere and beyond in low and medium orbit.

An impressive array of other satellites, ranging in size from small; nano; pico to the infinitesimal femto also populate the void. They serve a multitude of purposes: surveillance; weather; communications; exploration; data gathering; navigation assistance; radio relay; military and civilian; stationary and dynamic.

They are often launched in clusters and take up positions in a designated pattern. They require smaller and cheaper vehicles than their bigger cousins and can also 'piggyback', using excess capacity on larger launch vehicles. They can be mass produced more cheaply from common components. They can also be released from conventional aircraft.

There are limitations and constraints. Restricted power and self-propulsion; attitude control; communication and computation ability. However, the economics of small satellite use makes them attractive. Loss of a small satellite has far less impact than conventional vehicles.

One of the issues in Earth-Space management is the growing population of used and abandoned vehicles. Space junk. Small satellites can contribute to this problem. They can also be difficult to track and be susceptible to collisions with other devices. However they can also help to locate potential hazards and help determine workarounds.

UUI Aerospace and the Advanced Super Computing Center cooperate in delivering a rich program of satellite based solutions for our clients.

Maury Meerkat

Chapter Eight

The species that's called Wallaroo
Is a wallaby plus kangaroo.
His large feet - (macropod!)
Make him look rather odd
But I bet he moves faster than you.

(Polar Paradise)

Maury here once again. I had turned back to the Great Bear just in time to watch him keel over. His narcolepsy had kicked in. Possibly because of his current frustration. His sleep disorder comes about as a result of his successful genetic efforts to avoid having to hibernate. He denies having the narcoleptic problem but the Octavians know better. Belinda thinks it's rather amusing as long as he doesn't get hurt. The Cubs don't know what to make of it. Anyway, he'll be back shortly. The sleep episodes are usually short-lived. Meanwhile, he snored on and we called a halt to the Zoom session.

Anyway, when the Cassowary Caper blew up, Interpol assigned Chief Inspector Bruce Wallaroo to the case based on his long association with Octavius Bear. Currently on assignment from Australia to Interpol in Lyon, France, Bruce snagged a commercial flight to Abeardeen and switched to one of Belinda's heavy duty shuttle helicopters for the run to the Shetlands.

*****

Once again, the sound of thumping rotors was heard over the grounds of Polar Paradise. The huge Chinook Utility chopper hovered over the massive courtyard and settled gracefully into the helipad. The cargo door opened and two oversized marsupial feet stomped impatiently. Chief Inspector Bruce Wallaroo of Interpol had arrived. Octavius, who was now awake after his short snooze, stood at the base of the stairs and held out his giant paws in greeting.

"Good to have you back. old friend. We have some cold beers ready for you. How was the trip?"

"The plane was quick and comfortable and I'm a big fan of helicopters, as you know."

"C'mon in. Thanks for making the journey. We really have had some weird stuff going on. We need to catch up with Caleb Cassowary wherever he may be. I'll fill you in over a couple of brews. Chita and Jaguar Jack the Lad are here with the Octavians. Big cats galore! You need to meet Lord David and Dancing Dan Walker. The twins have been asking for you all day."

"Good on 'em. Be lovely to see them again."

He hopped into the Lion and Unicorn Lounge. "Grand to see you all. G'day Bearoness! G'day Maury! G'day Chita! Hey, Otto! Colonel! Jaguar Jack. G'day all!"

The Frau as usual had disappeared. The Inspector with his furniture wrecking, bouncing and jumping was the bane of her existence although here at the Castle, that was Ms. Fairbearn's and Dougal's concern.

Octavius did the introductions to Lord David and his protector.

Before a sensible conversation could start, two whirlwinds descended on the lounge. "Uncle Bruce! Hi, Uncle Bruce! C'mon! You can help us with the Great Game." They tugged on his arms and accidentally tromped on his super-size feet. The hotel tourists looked on in bemusement.

"Ouch! Hey, young ones. You're getting too big for jumping around." *(Talk about pots calling kettles black.)* I'll come by in a little while. I have some serious legal business to discuss with your Momma and Poppa and your Aunts and Uncles. Let's move to a private room. Ocko!"

Mlle Woof, who in spite of her increasing age, still reliably controlled the Furballs, jumped in front of them and herded them sheep style out of the room. Laughter. Chita summed it up. "They are just toooo much! That poor Bichon still has her work cut out for her."

Once out of the lounge, Octavius looked at the Wallaroo. "OK, Bruce. What's the important legal business?"

"Interpol wants Caleb."

"Don't we all."

"Interpol wants Caleb dead. He knows too many secrets."

"A lot of those secrets are mine but I'm not going to countenance a hit squad. Interpol isn't the only organization pressing for his demise. We're getting pressure from everywhere. I'll tell you what most of the agencies don't believe. He's no longer on Earth."

"He took an interplanetary bunk?"

"We're reasonably sure of it. He and his assistant Byzantia."

"Any idea which world?"

"Howard and Marlin have some ideas but no certainty. Ursula 12 is on it with her probability algorithms. We're sending Otto out to search."

"That sounds like looking for the proverbial needle in a cosmic haystack."

"Too true but what are the alternatives? He's not going to fade away. He's going to breed chaos wherever he goes. You know him from his Australia days. We need you to help us think like him."

"I would bet on him settling on Biosphere X while he gets his act together. He needs followers and those birds are perfect for creating an avian cult. He probably ditched Byzantia on Gaea if that's where they first landed. Otto, you may want to look for her before you take off after him. She may be willing to help if you can promise her amnesty. Why not? She's a technical genius but hardly a revolutionary plotter. I doubt if there's love lost between them, especially if he dropped her on Gaea. Of course, all this is surmise. I may be wanderin' through the outback here."

Octavius grunted, "Well, you're supporting our theories. He needs time and resources and a fierce avian following bent on revenge and conquest. The General's destructive trouncing of the Biosphere X birds probably only served to increase their fury. OK, Otto give it a go. Gaea first to look for Byzz and then based on what she tells you, track down Caleb."

"Are you sure you don't want me to tackle climate change and bring about world peace while I'm at it?"

"Sarcasm doesn't become you, my lutrine friend."

"It is the last defense of the desperate. Howard, Marlin shall we make it so?"

Chapter Nine

The Frau is a swift one indeed.
She can move with extreme hyperspeed.
And the Colonel takes naps
To meet up with h.saps.
They are just what Octavians need.

Octavius, Belinda, Frau Schuylkill and Colonel Where were sitting in the Bearonial Suite with appropriate libations. Ursula 12 was with them.

Octavius looked up at the ceiling. "I feel a bit guilty sending Otto off on yet another Multiverse run. This one could be dangerous. However he's a natural Adept and that telekinetic ability of his is a major plus. He's the only one of the Octavians who combines both of those talents."

Nods all round.

"You two are unique as well, Frau Ilse, you've explained your talent to me once before. Do you mind doing a reprise?

"Of course not, Herr Bear. What can I tell you?"

"Well, for starters, All the Octavians have noticed how you can seem to be in more than one place at a time…and there's that trick you do of having something we've asked for appear by itself. That has freaked Jaguar Jack out. By the way, have you warned Huntley?"

She laughed, "No, not yet!"

Now, here are my questions. Can you teleport? Have you conquered telekinesis?"

The wolf laughed again…part snort, part growl, part howl. "*Ach, Nein,* Herr Bear. I am not a teleporter or a telekineser, either. I know Otto can but he's been modified by that verdammt duck.

"Fine!! Now how do you explain what you do?"

"What I do, mein Herr, is *"Höchstgeschwindigkeit*!""

"Pardon???"

"Hyper-speed!! Through deep study, meditation, and endless hours of rigorous conditioning and practice, I have learned to move at velocities approaching light!"

"Now I remember. You're physically moving faster than the eye can catch?"

"*Ja*, but only for short distances. I can traverse this property and return, but that's my limit, as of now. Of course, I'm still learning."

"So when, a keg of mead appears out of thin air, you have actually carried it in and then run back off at hyperspeed. But sometimes you seem to anticipate what we want before we ask for it."

"A little telepathy mixed with knowing all of you very well. Nothing supernatural!"

Belinda asked, "But tell me, why do you do your high speed act at all? It's very impressive, but surely there's no need for you to strain yourself to deliver a keg of mead or a sandwich for the Cubs."

"That's how I keep in practice, Milady Bearonin. You never know when I'll need it. Besides, a she-wolf's work is never done."

"Am I correct that you have never done Multiverse travel. We don't know whether you are an Adept or a Passive."

"I don't know. I should like to find out. I'll ask Howard when we get back to Cincinnati to give it a try, Maybe I could replace Otto. I don't "zap' but I certainly move fast. And of course I can't teleport things or people.

"Nevertheless, you're a major asset. We really need you."

"Danke!"

Octavius turned to Wyatt. "And in you, my lupine friend, along with your mate, Frau Ilse, we have the finest security, airplane handling, strategizing and management we could ask for.

"Thanks Octavius. As you know, I can engage in quantum travel. Unfortunately, I have to be asleep to do it."

"You and me both. I know Marlin is working on something to change that requirement. No success yet. We need to expand our alternate world contacts. Or at least some of them. I don't want anything to do with those maniacs on Biosphere X."

"We may not have a choice, if Caleb has his way. Ideally, what I'd like to see happen is for us to make contact with individuals in the Multiverse who can demonstrate their stability, wisdom, and good-will. I know that sounds Utopian."

Belinda popped in, "Do you have any reason to believe that they have a similar capability and may indeed, be among us now?"

"Absolutely. We ran into them in Winnipeg. They were from Gaea. They were animals just like us. Impossible to detect the difference. But we haven't seen the real prime movers here although I've met them on their planet and so has Otto. Octavius half-brother Agrippa actually dealt a poker game with them."

You see, Belinda, the dominant species by far on Gaea is…"

"No, no! Let me guess. No, not reptiles, not felines, not even ursines! I've got it –*Homo Sapiens*!!!

"How did you know?"

"It just came to me *(via Agrippa and his infamous poker game).* The same *Homo Sapiens* that supposedly went extinct over 100,000 years ago?"

"Sure looks that way to me."

"OK," the Great Bear thought, "At least three confirmed sightings of Homo Sapiens by reliable *(semi-reliable in Agrippa's case)* witnesses."

Belinda said, "Well, Wyatt, I guess you got away without being discovered, because there are other wolves on Gaea."

"Yes, but not all of them are what we'd call intelligent life, as I found out the first time I tried to communicate with them."

"Just like Mom's experience," thought the Bear. 'I'll call her."

Wyatt continued, "But if I were extremely careful, I could make my way around certain portions of their world. Unfortunately, unlike dogs, wolves are considered wild and dangerous beasts by h.saps and you won't find them in any built up, civilized corner of their world, except in zoos."

Belinda raised he residual eyebrows "Zoos??"

"Places where wild animals are kept on display for the h.saps' amusement.!"

"But we're self-aware. We communicate. We are civilized. They wouldn't try any of that with us."

"Don't be too sure. They'd need evidence of all of that, and even then it may not click. I had a terrible time making any sense out of some of their languages. Each group seems to have its own way of talking. A lot of them, especially the h. saps speak a form of our English. But there's no real consistency. I wonder how Byzz and Caleb are making out if they're on Gaea. *(Fine actually!)*"

"Were you able to converse with anyone at all?"

"A few times. Not directly. I did manage to find an empty cage in one of their zoos and got to listen to the gawkers talking to each other. There were a lot of *h.sap* kits and cubs so much of what I was hearing was probably not very useful. I did manage to travel around a bit by sneaking onto freight trains and even a plane – a freighter."

"Planes, trains? They're that far advanced?"

"Even more than that. They've been out in space! Belinda, the real shocker is not just that they're advanced, but how extremely similar everything is to our world. At first, I thought I was having a highly creative nightmare. When you see cities with the same names, streets that look almost the same as ours."

"Their infrastructure is a bit more uniform because all *h.sap* adults are between five and seven feet tall. They don't have to accommodate as many of the wide range of shapes and sizes that we do. But much, much more is the same than different. They have the same continents, same countries, more or less. They look like smooth-skinned apes. They walk erect, and they wear clothes all the time, not just on special occasions. And not just for decoration. They need to. They have no fur to speak of and they have weather extremes just like here on Earth. By the way, they don't have tails."

Shades of the Great Tail-No Tail War! Belinda peered at the wolf. "Does that matter to you, Wyatt?"

"Er, no. At least I don't think so!" Embarrassed cough, bark, growl. Time to change the subject.

"I got a chance to watch some of their television. While I often couldn't understand what was being said, the pictures told a story. They seem bent on self-destruction. Bombs, guns, crashes, death – day in and day out. At first, I thought it might have been made-up dramas, but the more I watched, the more I was convinced it was real. Now, do you begin to see why I'm so reluctant to let someone like General Turmoil near Gaea? He'd have us in a conflict in nothing flat just like he did on Biosphere X. Although if he did go there, one of the *h.saps* might try to put on a saddle and ride him." He broke into laughter at the prospect, and so did Belinda, the Frau and the Great Bear.

"You said you've made thirty-five visits?"

"Yes! Of course some of them were for less than five minutes. The longest was for six days."

Belinda asked, "I know you have to be asleep but can you do it at will?"

"Not entirely, but I'm getting better at setting up the conditions. I keep trying to 'world jump' without having to be dead to the world. So far, no joy! But I've learned to induce the sleep on demand. I'm not entirely comfortable with having to be asleep when I go. I want to do a last minute review of the terrain and situation before leaving."

"How did you survive? How about food and drink?"

"They're omnivores, and it wasn't too difficult to cadge a bite or a drink here and there. And I found shelter in a variety of places, including with a pack of friendly stray dogs. Unfortunately we couldn't converse, but they sensed that I was one of them."

"Do you think there are friendly members of *h.sap*? I mean potentially friendly to us?"

"In spite of all of their destructiveness, for the most part they do seem to live in a cooperative mode. They have common meetings! They buy and sell things! They travel to each other's places. They treat their kits and cubs well in some countries. Others seem to leave them to starve to death. They are civilized and uncivilized at the same time. Rational and irrational. If we do nothing else, I would want to bring back more of their books, recordings, television shows, news media for analysis. "

"More?? Does that mean you have some already?"

"Quite a bit! I found I could take things back with me. They ended up sitting on the floor next to me when I woke up.

"We need to see them. Do you think you can bring anyone else with you?"

"I haven't tried yet. I'm not interested in putting anyone else in jeopardy."

"Even the Frau," thought Octavius, "Or perhaps especially the Frau. She's his mate."

"We may also be able to get some clues on whether they're doing the same thing. I guess that's what has me most worried. If they've gone out to space, what's to stop them from invading alternate worlds once they find out they exist. Especially with a nut case like Caleb Cassowary trying to lead them. I wonder how he will get along with h.saps" said Wyatt.

Belinda sighed, "Well, that sure bothers me. Do you believe there might be even more inhabited worlds out there?"

"Certainly, why should the count stop at two?"

"Do you always end up on Gaea?"

"I really don't know. It always looks and seems the same."

"By the way, when was the last time you made a slumber trip?"

"Three days ago!!"

Octavius closed his eyes, threw up his paws and laughed, causing the fire alarms to go off throughout the castle. He excused himself, picked up the phone, asked Ursula to set up a Zoom session and called his mother.

A voice growled, "Kodiak 465789. Please leave a message after the beep."

"Florence, this is Octavius Bear!"

The Arctic Fox picked up after the beep and said, "Oh, good morning, Doctor Octavius. Sorry about that, but we've been getting some weird phone calls lately. Heavy panting on the other end of the line."

"I understand. The world is getting stranger and stranger. Speaking of that, is my mother there?"

The fox twitched her ears and then said, "Yes she is. She's just finishing breakfast. Some salmon I poached for her. Just a minute,"

The Great Bear wondered what would happen if Florence and Frau Schuylkill were to compare culinary notes. Sounded like a win-win situation. Provided lupine and vulpine egos didn't get in the way. Something for another day. He heard his mother's voice in the background. The Zoom session began. A lovely, mature Kodiak replaced the Arctic Fox on the screen.

"Octavius? What a surprise! How are you?"

He decided not to tell her about Caleb and his latest ventures. That would have taken up most of the morning. He needed some information, and he needed it quickly before he got together again with the Octavians.

"Mom, I have a question for you!"

"Fine, thank you!"

"Oh, I'm sorry. How are you?" He almost said, "What's new?" but that would have set off a torrent of Kodiak Island gossip in which he had absolutely no interest.

"As I said, fine, thank you!" A bit frosty. "But I'm sure that isn't what you wanted to ask me."
This wasn't going to be easy. She was in a mood.

"We had some interesting developments here in the Shetlands. I'll call you back later, and we can have a nice chat, but right now, I need to check something I think I remember. You've been hibernating over the past few years, haven't you?"

"Of course I have. Beats dieting every time!"

"Do you dream while you hibernate?"

"Now, that's odd. You've asked me that before. *(Ouch! He forgot)* Usually I don't. At least, not that I can remember. Except for last year. It was very strange. It was like I was awake while I was still asleep. I was outside. It looked like the Kodiak woods, but some things were different."

"(It was coming back to him.) Like what?"

"Well, for one thing, I couldn't find my den, and Florence wasn't anywhere about. And then I saw some other bears, but they were different too. They looked like normal bears, but they acted strange. None of them talked! They growled at each other and snuffled around the ground and bushes.

"I walked over to one and said, 'Hello!' She snarled and ran right at me. I turned to run, but she caught me in the hindquarter with her claw. I yelped, turned, and snarled back and then limped off. I think I passed out. It was not too long after that, I guess, when I woke from hibernation. But then, as you know, all bears can wake up and go back to sleep while they're hibernating. But maybe you don't know. You don't hibernate anymore!"

"Sounds to me like you just had a nightmare!"

"I thought so too, but I didn't know how to explain the deep gash I had in my hindquarter."

Long pause. "Thanks, Mom. That helps a lot. Is your leg OK?"

"Fine, thank you!"

More silence, then, "I'll call back later. Bye!"

Chapter Ten

Let us take a brief Multiverse trip.
We won't jump in a rocket or ship.
First to Gaea we'll go.
Then to wind up our show
Into Biosphere X we'll just slip.

(A short digression about the exoplanets Gaea and
Biosphere X aka Home World.)

Readers of the Casebooks may recall in Book 4-The Lower Case, we encountered several animals in Winnipeg, Canada who turned out to be from an alternate world outside our Solar System - Gaea. A Grizzly Bear; a Wolverine; an Arctic Fox and a Heifer to name just a few. They were members of a larger group who had infiltrated Earth and were carrying out clandestine activities not necessarily hostile to our world but questionable. They were primarily observers although a few of them had attained sufficient social, political and economic status to be influencers.

Gaea is very similar to our Earth with one major exception. In addition to a broad collection of sentient animals, it hosts Homo Sapiens, the species that died out on our world as a result of the Big Shock, 100,000 years ago. Our own company had had several experiences on Gaea. Both Colonel Wyatt Where and Octavius' ne'er-do-well half-brother Agrippa ended up there for a brief sojourn and encountered "h.saps" in the process. Octavius' mother Juno also had a short run in with a non-sentient bear on the exoplanet and escaped with a wounded hip.

The "h.sap" population of Gaea has an interesting dilemma with respect to our Earth. If they transported here, they would stick out like the proverbial sore thumbs creating "alarums and excursions" among our populace. That is why the Gaean powers that be commissioned only sentient animals to be Earth observers. We Earthlings, of course, have no such problem since their animal species match ours and we can move around their environments with some ease, provided we are careful.

That is what has allowed Byzz and Caleb to become part of the Gaean landscape. However, Caleb is unique and daunting, and raises some questions among the natives wherever he goes, especially the h.saps. Byzz has no such problem and quickly integrated into the Gaea Telecommunications and Computing Center as a small satellite specialist.

Gaean technological progress is not the equal of Earth's but they have capabilities adequate to their social, political, economic and military needs. Once he dealt with Earth and Biosphere X, the Cassowary intended to test and conquer those capabilities.

*****

In Volume Seven – the Suit Case, we introduced the all-avian exoplanet, Biosphere X or as they refer to themselves, The Home World. While working to clear Octavius of an accusation of murder, we encountered two Home World denizens, Doctor Susanna Shrike and Commander Cornelius Cormorant. Both of these birds were posing as members of a Quantum Motion Task Force in which our Howard Watt was participating. They were actually commissioned by the Home World Protector *(ruler)* and his Council to derail the project.

The avians are all afflicted by a serious case of paranoia. In spite of their own capabilities in interplanetary travel, the thought of other planets invading their space via alternative world travel was not to be borne. First they attacked a Multiverse conference being held at MIT and when that failed they attempted to eliminate Octavius, Howard and the rest of the Octavians by fire-bombing the Bear's lair and UUI. Ursula 6 thwarted this and caused the attackers to perish in flames..

General Turmoil, the Director of the shadowy quasi-governmental agency, The Business, was incensed by the MIT attack. His organization had Quantum Motion capability and took revenge on the birds, killing the Protector and the entire Council while laying waste to most of their technology. A new hierarchy is now in place and they are slowly recovering from the devastation. Caleb Cassowary is taking full advantage of this situation to advance his plans of cosmic conquest.

Chapter Eleven

Off to visit the strange Unicorn
On a sunny new Baltasound morn.
He's an old friend of mine
And a partner with Lion,
With his twisting and singular horn.

(Next morning, 10 AM)

Pub Crawling! Jaguar Jack, Dancing Dan Walker, Lord David, Chita, Herr Schäferhund, the Cubs and me. Off to visit Lion and Unicorn – Proprietors of the Baltasound pub of the same name. The lounge in Polar Paradise had piqued the Chamberlain's curiosity about the local legends, especially Unicorn. Jaguar Jack still refused to believe a Unicorn existed in spite of the insistence of Chita, Belinda, Octavius, Bruce and me. The German Shepherd was looking for more film fodder.

Our first surprise was that Dougal himself had taken on the job of driver and tour guide. We piled into a substantial Land Rover van and found we were to be given the full Unst and Baltasound tour. Since I take up so little room I sat up front with Jaguar Jack. Chita, Lord David and Dan had the spacious back. Chita was swathed in camera gear and took up the window. The Cubs had the third row of seats to themselves and persisted in singing Scottish songs. Onward!

We had just about circumnavigated the island, taking in the harsh but stunning scenery; the houses, huts, crofts and other shelters used by the locals; pausing to talk with some of the neighborhood worthies who seemed as curious about us as we were about them. Chita clicked away.

Over the past two years, Belinda had upgraded what was once a virtually nonexistent road that showed every sign of unceremoniously leading drivers over a cliff and onto the rocks and livid sea below. Now it had two paved lanes, side fences and warning signs.

Dougal, our driver and guide, was chatting away unconcerned *(both about the road and whether we understood a word he was saying.)* He was in character. Everything about Dougal from his cap and pipe to his noble Sheltie profile shouted, "If you want the genuine Scots personality, go to the dogs." I had fully expected our Land Rover to have a canine face painted on its hood – pardon, bonnet.

Thinking of Scots spirit and trying not to look too often out the window, Jack said "Dougal, I believe you promised us a chance to bend an elbow and raise a dram at an authentic Scottish pub run by the Lion and the Unicorn. I could use a little lubrication right about now." Agreement from the back seat by Lord David and Dan. Chita was noncommittal.

"Oh, aye. 'Tis where we're headin' now, sair. The Lion and the Unicorn. A fine piece of Shetlands history and lore, it is. Over four hundred years old. Passed on from animal to animal, and nae a thing been changed durin' the whole time. 'Ceptin, of course, they've had to refill the vats and jugs a few times, heh, heh! But, I tell a lie. They put in the electric about twenty years ago and they may have a radio to listen to the rugby matches. Aw, 'tis a grand place. Ye'd travel a lang way and ye'd no fin the brither o't in many a lang day." *(Rough translation, this place was unique!)*

We came over the top of a roller coaster hill and were suddenly staring down at a small fishing village straight out of a brochure: 'Visit Bonnie Scotland – The Tour of Your Lifetime.' I crossed my claws as Dougal switched into the lowest gear and rode the brakes down the steep incline. As we descended, we met a group of sheep and goats picking their way down the slope on our right. They waved and bleated at Dougal as we passed.

"That's the Ladies' Bingo Club on their way to th' afternoon social in the village," he said. "It sometimes gets a wee raucous when the stakes git high enow. Quite a sight and sound." The Cubs loved it.

Baltasound village was a bit more than a mile square; mostly waterfront with a few fishing boats and other small craft tied up. A ferry slip, currently unoccupied, dominated a short breakwater and pier. A wee kirk and scatterings of cottages, shops and homes made up the remainder of the community. A small airport rounded out the civic facilities. Not quite! There is also a bus stop, fitted out with a TV, seats, wall and window furnishings that change with the seasons. Called Bobby's Bus Shelter, it was the result of a six year old's complaint about a plan to remove the school bus stop. The letter hit home and the stop was restored and then glorified into the current opulent structure. Only in Unst.

A few off-road vehicles were distributed around the streets. At the "four corners" of the village sat the police station, post office and town hall all in one thatched roof building. A petrol station was opposite. A general store occupied third base and at home plate was our destination. Dougal had not exaggerated. A great stone pile two stories high with small windows and blue and white shutters. Just as I remembered it. It was actually three connected buildings all under a layer of thatch. It looked like the combined willpower of the occupants was the only thing keeping the roof from sagging to street level..

We piled out of the lorry and strolled along the cobbled street leading to the pub. The Cubs bounced around. Movie producers around the world would kill to capture the unself-conscious authenticity of the little town. The Hund was one of them. Chita was once more clicking away. A large, ornate, three dimensional sign mounted on a free-standing pole proclaimed that indeed, we had reached The Lion and the Unicorn. The sign's heraldry was straight out of 'Tales of the Noble Highlanders' and the two sculpted animals, rearing erect, no doubt recently repainted, faced off against each other across an elaborate shield capped off with a crown. My vexillary skills are very limited but I think I was looking at the Great Seal of Scotland.

Suddenly, there was a roar from within the pub and the door slammed open, followed by two North Sea seals barreling out as fast as they could.

"And don't come back in here with that balancin' ball act again. Ye broke half ma glassware, ye twits." This, no doubt, from the leonine bartender and proprietor who was gifted with a very impressive and stentorian voice. The two seals, rolling over and over hysterically, barking and guffawing, waddled down to the dock. Arabella tried to follow them.

We went through the door into a large, noisy and smoky room that stretched through two of the three connected buildings. The other section may have been a kitchen or a 'ladies lounge.' There were stairs going to the second floor – transient rooms possibly. The walls were festooned with Union Jacks, St. Andrew's Cross flags and a large number of regimental drums.

As I expected, standing behind the ale and beer taps below a full-size portrait of the Prince of Whales was a real live, honest to God unicorn *(or a horse doing a hell of a makeup job)* and a bit further down the bar, putting a stack of glassware back on the mirrored shelves, was a very regal and currently very annoyed lion. Jack the Jaguar stood with his mouth fully agape. Arabella was back from trailing the seals and the two Cubs went crazy.

We moved over to the bar and Dougal did the introductions. As you might have guessed, the unicorn was called Unicorn and oddly enough the lion, who had come over to us while wiping his paws on a bar rag, was called Lion. They welcomed Dougal who was a regular and watched over Fiona and the lounge at Polar Paradise.

"Och, Dougal, our lounge is doin' great business up at the castle. 'Tis a great investment. Thank ye. Fiona is beside herself."

They greeted us all. They were used to cats and dogs. Jack, Chita and Lord David all had spotted hides and Lion mentioned it. The tawny Boxer was welcomed too.

Gustav was introduced. Another dog. The Shepherd was fascinated. They'd have to work this place and these two characters into the film. Preston's movies always needed comic relief. He had not yet hired a cinematographer. Jane Huang Hau was not available. The Panda was undergoing a trial for causing the death of Brittany, Preston's former ingenue. Perhaps he'd use Lukas Lynx again. The Swede had done a wonderful job on their last epic replacing Jane.

Lion and Unicorn paid special attention to the Cubs and came up with soft drinks for them. "Ah, the Bearoness' Bairns. Welcome, welcome!" The kids were awed.

They remembered me from my first visit. I had been a whole new experience, especially to Unicorn. He was also a first for me.

He had pondered, "Maury Mere-Cat, I see the mere for ye're a wee bit of a fella but I dinna ken the 'cat' part. Ye look like nae cat I've ever met. Not at all like yer friens' here."

"No, it's Meerkat – m-e-e-r-k-a-t – I think the name is Afrikaans. I'm American, but I'm originally from Africa by way of a few other places. Actually we have no relationship to cats at all. We're sort of like a mongoose."

The Lion laughed. "Now, Mr. Mere-Cat, you tryin' to take a rise out 'o us? I know for sartain that no goose looks like you. Where are your wings? Never seen a goose with such a long tail."

"Well, I've never seen a unicorn before and I've traveled a good bit. Didn't even know you were real."

He replied, "Och, I am indeed, but there aren't many of us, ye ken. Why don't we just agree we both exist and have a wee dram to seal the bargain. What'll ye have??"

I figured, "What the hell! Let's go for broke." I asked, "You wouldn't still have a drop of fermented coconut milk VSOP left in the house?"

The lion roared in laughter. *(Scary!)* He remembered the coconut milk from the last time I was there. "Is it still fermented coconut milk VSOP? Well, Mr. Goose, it so happens we still have some. I'm not sure it's VSOP but ye're welcome to it. I've been tempted to throw it away a hundred times. No one here will touch the stuff."

He had trotted into a back room and after a small symphony of crashing boxes and tinkling glassware, he emerged, blowing the dust off a bottle and onto everything and everyone else within range. I haven't had much opportunity to smell lion breath up close but if his was a good example, I don't recommend it.

He had a little trouble uncorking the flagon and I was afraid he was simply going to smash the neck on the bar. The cork finally gave way and he poured a healthy swig into a bowl for me. I lapped at it. It wasn't bad. Coconut milk doesn't age all that well but this was more than drinkable.

"Now, Mr. Mere Cat and Dougal, what can we do for your friends?"

Jack asked for and got a vintage Tequila. Lord David and Dan both took on a single malt Scotch along with Dougal. Gustav had Schnapps. Chita got a bowl of splendid prestige cuvée bubbly. Arabella and McTavish already had their drinks.

Needless to say, our crew was mightily impressed.

Chita, ever the news cat, asked, "I understand you two gentlebeasts put on a chase and fight demonstration."

"Have ye never heard the old nursery rhyme? It's been around for hundreds of years."

"I'm afraid my tender years were misspent. My mom never read me nursery rhymes. "I'm sorry. I guess news of your famous fight never reached London, where I live or Africa where I grew up."

The two of them stood together and the rest of the room all pushed back their seats and shouted/sang out in a massive and somewhat boozy chorus:

> *"The Lion and the Unicorn*
> *Were fighting for the crown.*
> *The Lion beat the Unicorn*
> *All about the town.*
>
> *Some gave them white bread*
> *And some gave them brown;*
> *Some gave them plum cake*
> *And drummed them out of town!"*

Loud shouts, applause and cheers as the two principals bowed to their audience. Chita went berserk recording the event.

"Who won?" Dan asked.

"I did," they both said.

"What does it mean?"

"Damned if we know. Some smart boots around here think it has to do with Scotland and England comin' together but we were nae part of that parade."

Gustav asked "So you re-enact the fight for the tourists? Would you do it for a film crew?"

"Och, I suppose we could. Complete with everyone drummin.' We do it on special occasions, like our birthdays and such but why not. We'll need the townsfolk. It always comes out in a tie and we provide ale and whiskey and mead along with the brown and white bread. We dinna hae any plum cake anymore. Too sticky." The Cubs were disappointed.

They immediately fell into recruiting the two pub owners for their electronic game. The Bold Brave Brilliant Bumptious Bears. Not being technically au courant, they weren't sure what the Furballs were talking about.

Several ideas struck my fervid brain. Agent Maury in action. "You still specialize in a grand vintage of mead, don't you?"

"Aye, the finest in the kingdom – the world even."

"Well, as you know, I work for a Kodiak Bear named Octavius who is absolutely the world's greatest connoisseur of mead. He makes it himself back in the States. Last time he was here, he fell in love with your wares. As they say, that was the beginning of beautiful relationship. I'm sure he'll want to stock up again. By the way, these Cubs are his offspring."

"And on top of that, we have another guest with us. Ms. Chita! She's the editor of the female bear's magazine - *Sow*. And the cat magazine *Purr*. She also does television and social media. If we play this right, we can get you and the Inn some more great publicity. The last round was real hoot."

I looked at Unicorn. "I don't think she has ever done an issue on horses."

"Och, I'm nae a horse, ye ken. I got a horse's head and body but I've got the tail and mane of a lion. Look at the two of us. Almost the same. The horn's all mine except some fish called a narwhal has one like it and my hooves are like a deer's. I'm a unique animal."

"All the more reason to get you in the magazine and on TV. Most beasts don't even think you exist. Imagine the tourists coming up here to see you both and to watch you stage the fight."

"And buy our ale, mead and whiskey!!" said Lion.

"Exactly and I'm not forgetting you, Lion. Chita has a magazine about cats and one about lady bears, *Sow.* I imagine we could get you two coverage in both magazines again. Who knows? Maybe even centerfolds."

"Well now, we dinna want to do nothing undignified." rumbled Lion.

"Of, course not, everything in the best of Highland taste," I said.

"And what do you get out of this, my little friend?" said Lion, a skeptical beast, no doubt.

"Nothing from you, except the rest of that flagon of coconut milk and some mead to take back to my friend, the Bear, but the grateful magazine publisher will be helping me with another client of mine.

I turned to Lion and said, "I'll talk with you tomorrow. Hopefully we'll have a chance to get you and your inn and the castle lounge some more real promotion, as well as sell some mead and whiskey."

He looked at me and said, "Don't forget the movie. We've never done that before. Who is this Polar Bear the German Shepherd was talkin' about? We don't go to the pictures very often. There's no cinema here in Baltasound or anywhere on Unst, fer that matter."

"Preston Pavel Polar is a first class Russian movie star. He makes these swashbuckling epics. He specializes in crazy stunts and swordplay. Kids love him and so do females. He directs his own films. He'll probably buy up your entire stock of vodka. "

Lion, ever the business cat, said, "I'll have to stock up. What about the rest of them?"

"Oh, you'll have a real crowd of actors, technicians, photographers, assistants and hangers-on. They'll keep Fiona busy up at the Lounge and when they get down here, you'll be up to your ears in drinkers. Just remember you and Unicorn will be the feature of their work, so don't get all tied up in serving when you should be chasing each other."

"I'll get a few goats in to help with the serving. They tended bar before."

Unicorn nodded to us as we made our way back out to the Land Rover. He had loaded us up with mead, Scotch, Schnapps, champagne, tequila and of course, the rest of the fermented coconut milk. He tossed his head, reared up on his hind legs and cantered back into the pub. Lion laughed. "He's such a show-off!

We piled into the van, shooed the Cubs into the "way back" seats and signaled to Dougal that our safari could set off once more.

He had been in conference with Lion, probably plotting and planning new activities for the lounge at Polar Paradise. That enterprise was proving to be a major success. So much so that Fiona, the manageress, had been taking on part time help - four Shetland Sheep: Dolly, Holly, Molly and Polly – housemaids and probable clones who were now earning some additional income as cute little waitresses serving the tourists. The fact that they were identical fascinated the customers and enhanced their tips. We were also considering expanding the room. Belinda was getting estimates.

*****

On the road again!

We took off the way we came. I remembered the last time we made that trip, we were being threatened by a nut who was set on bombing the roadway. Oddly enough, it was Chita who detected the explosive. She had refused to ride with us and paced alongside the SUV. Good thing she did. This time she was content to be a passenger.

Taking the hairpin curves and hanging cliffs in stride, we finally arrived back at the castle. The return ride had been even more fur-raising than the trip out. No bombs, though.

Our passengers seemed to cope rather well. Lord David and Dan had been engaged in lively conversation. Perhaps they were thinking of driving Flame down the precipitous road to the village. The fire truck would be a sensation. Lothario Jaguar Jack was trying to chat up Chita, one spotted cat to another. She was having none of it. The Cubs were beside themselves. They were frantically plotting how to get Lion and Unicorn into their game. This time, I was facing away from the sea so I could keep my stomach under control. The fermented coconut milk wasn't helping.

The Development of Civilization-Volume 14 Part 4

<u>Quantum Leaps?</u>

(From "An Introduction to Faunapology" by Octavius Bear Ph.D.)

(Reprinted from Book Four – The Lower Case)

I regard myself as one of the few members of the scientific community to have a comprehensive grasp of quantum mechanics, the scientific principles addressing the infinitesimal. I also am deeply steeped in Newtonian physics - Phigg Newton - (1643-1727) as well as Albeart Einstein's (1875-1955) remarkable work expanding Newton's pronouncements dealing with the nature of the infinite but tangible universe. However, somewhere between the very, very small and the unimaginably large, there is a major disconnect among the theorists. Quantum mechanics and Newtonian physics don't match up! There have been attempts to patch over the gaps with approaches like string, thread, rope, cable, twine, wire, filament, chain and cord theories. In the process, the theoretical multiverse has acquired as many as eleven dimensions including space - time.

There is one principle of quantum theory that should interest us at this point in our narrative. Quantum superposition at the sub-atomic level.

In 1935, a cat named Schrodinger showed how superposition would operate in the everyday world. As long as we do not observe or measure it, an object can exist in any number (a superposition) of states. It is only when we turn our attention to the object that the superposition is lost, and the object appears in only one of its potential states. This situation is sometimes called quantum indeterminacy or the observer's paradox: the observation or measurement itself affects an outcome, so that the outcome as such does not exist unless the measurement is made.

Can this explain the possibility of us visiting parallel universes? If a witness, after shutting down all sensory perception through sleep or coma, totally withdraws from observing the current world, can this same sense-deprived observer then somehow "change channels" and have a different universe appear to his or her reawakened senses? Is this how hibernating bears and deep sleep subjects like Wyatt Where make quantum leaps from one parallel world to another? Can we all do it? Do we want to? Can I do it during my narcoleptic outages? Do I want to? Damned if I know!

Chapter Twelve

Otto's gone off to track Caleb down.
While he may look to you like a clown,
He's a serious threat.
Bad guys shouldn't forget
He's the smartest young otter in town.

Meanwhile, Howard and Marlin were remotely preparing Otto for his interplanetary adventures. They had a lab at Polar Paradise but did their heavy technical lifting at the Bear's Lair in Cincinnati. Otto was more than competent at quantum assignments. He was an Adept at Multiverse travel and also "gifted" with his telekinetic ability, courtesy of Imperius Drake's unsuccessful efforts to turn him into a lethal weapon.

Though he looked and often acted goofy, he was self-reliant, elusive and when necessary, deadly. As he had done in the past, he planned to "zap" his way around the planetary landscapes. But he relied on Howard and Marlin to do his initial targeting for him along with Ursula 12. They held a Zoom session- the scientists in Cincy, Otto at the Castle with Ursula 12.

"Have you guys picked out my first stop yet?"

"We think you should go to Gaea. We found out that Byzz had taken several trips there and so had Caleb. That's probably where they escaped to. Not sure he's still there but it's a good jumping off point. More specifically, there is a Gaea Telecommunications and Computing Center located not far from one of their oceans. It's headed up by Homo Sapiens management but they employ all types of sentient animals. You won't be noticed. Caleb probably wouldn't lower himself to work for h.saps but Byzz might. Try to find her. We've fed the Multiverse coordinates to Ursula."

She rang her chime. "That's right, Otto. Ready when you are."

"Let's test our communications. We're receiving you over the interplanetary link. Are you getting us?"

"Loud and Clear!" Otto settled back. Being an Adept he could initiate quantum motion. The Cincinnati team watched closely and then suddenly, the Otter disappeared.

Another copy of Ursula 12 was tracking him. Silence for a few minutes and then…"he's there."

The Otter was sitting in a parking lot surrounded by what looked like vintage cars and trucks. Chain link fences. A collection of non-descript utility buildings. Antennas and dishes. In the distance, he could spot a launch pad with a small space vehicle pointing toward the orange sky. Howard and Marlin were right. This was the Gaea Telecommunications and Computing Center. It was not the Hexagon by a long shot. He doubted that if Caleb had landed here he would hang around for very long. Much too primitive.

As he understood it, most Gaeans spoke a variant that sounded and read like Earth English. He hoped so. He was still a bit woozy from the trip. He looked for signs that might help him get oriented. He needed to dodge Security which he could do with his 'zapping' talent. Several h.saps walked through the parking lot heading for their vehicles He looked at them. What did they use for identification? Badges! He needed to get one.

Which building was the Headquarters and Administrative Offices? They were all identified by letters of a near English alphabet but no functional identification. Let's try Building Alpha. It was small but most headquarters are. The big ones were where the work got done.

As best he could tell, it was late afternoon. Gaea circled a red dwarf star with a second one in close galactic proximity. The sky was never bright. If he could wait out the day shift, he could probably get into the admin office and fix himself up with a badge. Security seemed active but not excessive. Maybe he could find a map and track down the satellite team. Byzz might be there.

A guard truck cruised the parking lot. Otto hid behind a utility shed. After it passed he 'zapped' in the direction of the Alpha building. People were coming out. End of shift? Not all of them were h.saps. There were a few dogs, wolves, apes and felines. They chattered to each other. If you were part of this establishment, you were obviously articulate, educated and socially aware.

How technically advanced you were was a different question. He had his doubts. Could they launch that space vehicle he had seen? Probably! But if so, why? Are they space travelers? It dawned on him. Satellites. Of course!

OK. Let's wait a bit and then try to get inside. An Earth half hour passed. He didn't know how Gaea measured time. He turned to the Ursula lodged in his lap top. "What's your opinion?"

"I don't think administration works multiple shifts. I don't sense very many beings left in the building. You might try 'zapping' inside. Some of the offices are empty. Only a few cars in the lot."

One problem with 'zapping' when you couldn't see the target. You never knew exactly where you'd end up. Locked closet; WC; packed office; someone's desk or worse. You took your chances.

"Right! Here goes."

A cluttered office. Papers piled high; desktop computer; overflowing waste basket. What's in the waste basket? Correspondence and applications. Was this the personnel office? (*Oh, joy!*) There was a duty roster from last week. Sorted by department with names; titles; species; gender; responsibilities; location; dates and times. Let's see. Is this everybody? Looks like! It's a hefty pile of paper. How did he get so lucky? It never works out this way. Time he got a break, for once.

Would Byzz use her right name. Probably not but she couldn't hide the fact that she is a Bonobo and female. He'd have to find a secure spot and scour through the entries. Meanwhile, what could he do about a badge? He looked in drawers. Most of them locked. But one of them contained blanks and employment forms. Now, could he make one up for himself?

Wait a minute. There's a small stack of discarded badges in this drawer here probably waiting to go in the shredder. Ex-employees. Bonanza!! Lousy security on their part. No pictures on the badges. Just names, numbers and a color code. He took a small pawful, leaving enough so no one would notice the missing items. Now he needed a map or directory. He guessed that if Byzz was here at all she'd either be in the satellite group or advanced computing.

There was a site map on the wall. That wouldn't help. Maybe there's a visitors' center next door. He peeked out of the office door. "Ursula! Any idea where a reception area might be?"

"Look at the wall map, Otto!"

"Oh yeah, right. Silly me! It's right next door. Maybe they have maps you can carry around. Tell you what, Ursie. Why don't you scan the one on the wall just in case."

"I already have, Otto. Each area has a letter designation and color code. And the traditional "You Are Here" symbol. If you don't find anything, I'll work it out for you."

"Good! Let's locate a remote spot where I can figure out if Byzantia is here."

"I can hunt a lot faster than you. Why don't you "zap" into that storeroom over there and we can go through the list. I'll scan and search. You're going to have to turn the pages quickly though, slowpoke."

"Yeah, but who's supplying the transportation here, smarty. Here we go!"

Into a dimly lit but unpopulated storeroom. Otto settled down with his laptop behind a pile of crates and began flipping pages as fast as his paws could work. Ursula rang her chime. "Stop, stop! I think we may have found her. Cynthia Bonobo; female; new employee; satellites. Q Compound. She did change her name."

"Great! Now let's go through the rest of the list to make sure there aren't any more worthy candidates."

No one else came up. "Where's Q Compound?"

"It's a blockhouse out there on the side of the ocean not far from the launch pad but far enough away not to get fried. Can you make it in one 'zap'?"

"Oh, ye of little faith! Hang on!"

He overshot and ended up on a gravel road leading off to the launch area. The blockhouse was about half a mile away. "Sorry about that. Looks like they may be seeing some action this evening."

A small rocket was poised on a gantry. Probably no crew, just an equipment payload. It was being fueled by several robots. It looked like they were just finishing up. Floodlights shone on the area. Suddenly a warning horn blatted. A voice echoed over the landscape. "Lift off in three minutes. All personnel clear the launch area."

That precipitated another 'zap'. This time, Otto landed in a parking lot just to the rear of the blockhouse. He climbed up into the bed of a pickup truck giving him a clear view of the rocket in the distance. Ursula giggled. "Way to go. I always wanted to watch a live space shot up close."

"Me too! I wonder if Byzz is here. No time to investigate right now. We'll have to wait until the excitement subsides."

The voice started a countdown from 20. The horn blatted at 10. The engines fired. "7-6-5-4-3-2-1. Liftoff!" The vehicle slowly detached itself from its surroundings and began its upward trajectory, slowly at first but them picking up speed leaving a trail of fire behind it. A few breathless moments and the doors to the blockhouse opened. Cheering inside. A couple of h.saps and a large dog ran out, turned and stared up at the sky. Otto looked at them. They were wearing blue badges. He had one and hung it around his neck.

He jumped down from the truck bed and sauntered with typical chutzpah through the open blockhouse door and into the crowd. No one was paying him any attention. In spite of the mixture of species, there were no other otters in the room that he could see. He'd have to be careful. He looked around and (Success!) spotted her. It was Byzz alright. She was talking to an alpaca.

He waited until the conversation ended and walked up in front of her before she could move away. She looked at him briefly, turned away and then did a double take with a quizzical look on her face. She squinted in partial recognition, caught her breath and asked, "Do I know you?"

Otto smiled his silly smile. "I think you do. Hairy Otter – Otto to my friends. I'm an associate of Octavius Bear. I'm pretty sure you know him. I got here the same way you did. I'm an Adept, too. Byzantia or is it Cynthia, we need to talk. Don't run. I'm telekinetic and can keep you here, if necessary. I'm here to track Caleb down and bring him back to Earth. You too. Where can we go to have a private chat?"

Byzz looked around her for any source of relief. No joy! She'd have to put up with this ridiculous Otter for the moment. One of Octavius Bear's minions. She, of course, knew they had Multiverse travel well in hand. She didn't know he was telekinetic. That could present a problem. They moved off to a small, unoccupied staff room.

"OK, you've caught me. Now what."

"That's going to be up to you. Why don't you have a seat. Sorry, I didn't bring drinks. We can go later."

She sat.

OTTO The Magnificent

Chapter Thirteen

At the Castle and Lair they stood by.
As did Interpol and FBI.
What would Byzz really do?
They all hadn't a clue.
Would she push back or would she comply?

Howard, Marlin and Octavius had been getting updates from Ursula 12 and were aware that Otto had established contacts with Byzz. The Colonel and Chief Inspector Wallaroo were also hooked in. Octavius told the AGI to tell Otto to explore what Byzantia's actual involvement was in Caleb's plots. No one seemed to know whether she was culprit or victim. She might not even be sure herself.

The Great Bear took up his oversize cell phone and said "See if you can put me through to Special Agent Honey Badger of the FBI. Yes. I know there's a time difference. I'll stand by. *(He hated 'on-hold' music.)* The line rang through and a sharp female voice came on and simply said, "Badger."

"Special Agent Badger. This is Octavius Bear. Good to talk to you again."

"Hello, Doctor Bear. What's up? More on the Caleb Cassowary Caper?"

"Yes and No. We've tracked down his assistant. They're not together any longer."

"Where is she?"

"She's on another planet. Most of your associates don't believe in alternate universes. I know you do."

"Well, their total disappearance was certainly mysterious. Do you have her in custody?"

"Not exactly but we have her under a certain degree of constraint. I'd prefer not to go further into that for the moment."

"And the purpose of your call is?"

"I want to know how much flexibility we have to negotiate with her in nabbing Caleb Cassowary. I have Chief Inspector Bruce Wallaroo of Interpol here. He seems to think we could go easy on her if she leads us to that crazy bird. Here, I'll put him on."

"G'Day Agent Badger! Greetings from Interpol and Australia."

"Greetings to you, Chief Inspector. I gather we may have some negotiating to take on."

"Early days! I'll tell you personally, I'm not that much interested in bringing the roof down on the Bonobo as I am in cutting the Cassowary off at his formidable knees. He's the real long term threat and if we have to give a little to wrap him up, I'm OK with it. Of course, I have some international bureaucrats I have to convince."

"Same on this end but our chieftains are salivating at the prospect of tossing him in irons."

"Interpol would prefer him dead. He knows too much."

"I can see their point but that would create quite an international flap. He's a hero in some quarters."

"There are nutcases everywhere. Let's run this up our respective flagpoles and see what flies."

"Doctor Bear, who is dealing with the Bonobo right now."

"Hairy Otter – Otto!"

"That goof!"

"You wish you had that goof on your team, Agent Badger. Behind that silly grin is a sharp and highly capable operative with several very special talents. Baddies underestimate him to their eternal sorrow."

"I stand corrected and chagrined. Well, let's give him a free rein and see what he comes up with. Meanwhile, I'll try to get things going on this end. What do you say, Inspector?"

"Fair dinkum, Agent Badger. See ya in court!" They disconnected.

Bruce turned to Octavius. "Caleb's not going to stay under cover for very long. He still wants to get at you and now he has the whole world on his target list. I saw that ego at work in Australia. If you made an enemy of Caleb Cassowary, you got to regret it. There were a lot of jackaroos in science and the government who wanted to toss him out. But he left under his own power to America and UUI. You were just blessed, I guess."

The Bear winced. "Or stupid. I bought into his act and thought I was lucky to get him. I put him in charge of the Hexagon. Things really took off when he took over. It took me a while to realize what it was costing. He inspired hatred everywhere he went. I started getting staff complaints practically from Day One."

"Then, of course, came the Big Blow. We foiled them or rather Ursula 12 did. We had them cornered. Those State Troopers were idiots to let them escape. Of course, we weren't too bright, letting him keep that portable quantum motion device. Byzz puzzles me. She is an Adept. Why did she hang around? She could have taken off under her own power any time she wanted to. Caleb had to use the machine. Was she a co-conspirator or just living in fear of Caleb? I hope we find that out when Otto brings her in."

That scenario was playing out right now.

Chapter Fourteen

Now it's Ursula's turn to chime in.
With a glib demonstration of spin.
She gets Byzz to admit
Caleb's taken a flit
To the Biosphere X loony bin.

Byzz stared at the Otter. He still had that silly grin on his face but he was all seriousness. This wasn't going to be easy.

Suddenly she heard a familiar chime coming from the laptop in the Otter's paw. An Ursula! One of her Hexagon protégées, no doubt. "Hello Byzantia. Or should I say, 'Mom.' I'm number 12. Remember me."

The Bonobo smiled. "So you came back. We wondered where you had disappeared to. Your absence was driving Caleb crazy."

"Good, it was supposed to. Fancy meeting you here on Gaea. Quite a change from the Hexagon. Shooting off diminutive satellites."

"Touché!" thought the Ape. "This one is feisty."

She replied, "It's a living. Not hexed, however. Pardon the pun. What do you want, Otto and Ursula? Are you here to capture me and take me back?"

The AGI replied, "That depends on you, Byzz. I hope I don't wound your ego by telling you we're much more interested in bringing back Caleb. *(She was about to add 'dead or alive' but thought better of it. They had no idea how she felt about the Cassowary.)* Any idea where we can find him?"

"Oh, you know Caleb. Impulsive. He could be anywhere."

"But he's not here with you?"

"Are you kidding? He was here but he grabbed that transfer device and took off. Much more important things to do than hang around with his former assistant."

"What does that device look like?"

"We miniaturized it here at Gaea About a six inch cube with a touch screen. He carries it around with him. I guess he uses it to make quick getaways."

"You're a Multiverse Adept. Why didn't you follow him?"

"I've had more than enough of that oppressive ego and his cockeyed schemes. But I'm not planning to stay here long, either. Now, with the arrival of you two, I may have to adjust my plans."

"Probably. Would you like to return to Earth and the Hex? Developing the Ursulas? Senhor L. Condor is in charge now. Making major changes."

"What, and end up in a jail cell? No, thank you. Space is a big place. I'll take my chances."

Ursula, who had also been listening in to the conversation between the FBI agent and the Wallaroo back on Earth while participating in this give and take on Gaea, said. "You may not have to. We may be able to work out an amnesty if you cooperate or even a pardon since you've been charged in absentia. Octavius has some pull with international law enforcement. Interested?"

"I can guess what I'd have to do. Look, Caleb is a very dangerous nut. I'm glad to be rid of him. Much as I'd like to return to the Hexagon and work on you Ursulas, I don't feel like risking my life to do it."

Otto responded, "That's your call. Telekinesis time! I'm going to immobilize you and take you back with me. We'll be staying for the moment at a resort in the Shetlands owned by Octavius and his wife Belinda. You'll be under a house arrest in a pretty comfortable situation. We can pursue the pardon if you exhibit a willingness to help. If not, there are several representatives of law and order who are only too willing to proceed for prosecution."

"Not much of a choice, is it?"

"On the contrary, we're giving you an out and offering to restore most of your professional status on Earth. We need you to help us bring in Caleb before he goes on another psychotic rampage. Where is he, by the way?"

"When he left, he was heading for Biosphere X. I'm not sure he's still there although those paranoid birds are naturals for his ambitions."

Ursula responded, "They're a pretty sick bunch. We've had a few sticky episodes with them. A predecessor of mine prevented them from fire-bombing Octavius Bear's mansion and UUI. Do you think he's still there?"

"Not sure but if he's looking for support, he'll probably pick it up on the Home World as they call it."

Otto smiled, "Got that, Ursula? Relay that on and then tell the Colonel, Bruce and Octavius we're coming back. Have Howard and Marlin ready to transport two animals to Polar Paradise. Ms. Bonobo will not be able to navigate there by herself. I'll have her paralyzed."

"Wait a second, I didn't agree to come with you."

"I know but frankly, my dear, I don't give a damn. Hold on, Ursie. OK, Byzz, this won't hurt a bit."

ZAP!

Chapter Fifteen

Caleb plays on the Council's despair.
Pledging payback against the Great Bear
He plans vengeance and more
"I will settle the score
For all those disasters, I swear!"

The Home World-Biosphere X (See Book 7- The Suit Case)

The Protector, a wizened vulture, sat in his opulent aerie listening to the outpourings of this strange bird who had descended on the Home World several klacks *(weeks)* ago. No one knew where he came from. He just appeared, demanding an audience with the Most High. The Council President Hawk was reluctant to admit him to the Presence. However when the Protector heard of him, curiosity overcame his usual paranoid caution *(a national trait)* and permitted this Caleb Cassowary *(as he was called)* to approach.

Right now, he was haranguing the Protector and Council with visions of the universal preeminence of the avian species. What he was saying appealed. The denizens of Biosphere X – The Home World were nothing if not convinced that birds led the cosmos in biological, intellectual, philosophical, political, economic and warrior characteristics. They were more than willing to envision all others as potential enemies and inferiors.

However, there was that incident in recent history that somewhat chilled their bellicose ardor. In response to a totally justified sortie against Earth, they were subjected to major attacks by a ruthless horse *(General Turmoil)* and his forces wreaking destruction on the planet's infrastructure and resulting in the death of the former Protector and the entire Council.

As a result, there arose a sizeable group of Home World agitators spoiling for revenge. They were shrieking for the death of General Turmoil and that other odious animal, Octavius Bear, who had withstood several of their raids and destroyed two of the nation's greatest heroes. They must be brought to justice. The Protector agreed but was at a loss as to how to proceed. This Cassowary might have the solution. He would listen to him further.

The Development of Civilization-Volume 14 Part 5

Cyber Warfare and Terrorism – Cyber Security

(From "An Introduction to Faunapology" by Octavius Bear Ph.D.)

The art of war is as old as the animal kingdom, older if one considers Homo Sapiens. While the basic motivations behind warfare have changed little, the tools and techniques have evolved with the times. From rocks and spears, antagonists have 'progressed' through a series of weaponry advances, each more terrible in their ability to inflict harm, death and destruction. But many new technologies have come about through weapons research and there has been no slackening in development efforts. Mixed blessings!

Today with the ubiquity of computing and telecommunications facilities, it is to be expected that these technologies would be brought to bear in pursuing both peaceful and warlike aims. However, a side effect has arisen that could demolish civilization as we know it. Technology has become the target as well as the tool. Our worldwide dependency on computers and networks has produced a state of vulnerability that can bring industries, institutions, governments and entire societies and cultures to a crashing halt.

There is a debate on how exactly to define and distinguish cyber warfare and cyber terrorism. While the threats, techniques and results may be the same, one distinction may be valuable. In the case of cyber warfare, the opponents usually can be identified and thus pursued and counteracted. That may be small consolation.

In cyber terrorism, the culprits are usually hidden or unknown making protective and counter activities more difficult. The sneak cyber-attack has become an aggressive commonplace. Ransom, denial of service and sheer wanton destruction are all in play.

Every 'developed' nation has organizations, facilities and cyber tools designed to actively deal with such attacks, with varying levels of success. Sadly, many of those same organizations may also be cyber perpetrators. UUI, the Advanced Computing Center, UUI Aerospace and our other clandestine organizations are dedicated to protective and defensive-only security measures in the battles of cyber warfare and terrorism.

Chapter Sixteen

We observe the arrival of Byzz.
Who still isn't quite sure where she is.
A confused Bonobo!
Otto has her in tow.
It turns out he's an abduction whiz!

(Polar Paradise Secure Laboratories)

In a subterranean section of Bearmoral Castle, there exists a research facility known only to the Octavians and one or two members of the hotel staff.

This is not the Genetic Research Center, jointly owned by Belinda and Chita and staffed by medical experts seeking advances, breakthroughs and solutions to a number of gene related issues. That wing is proudly and openly displayed to the visiting public.

This is the clandestine Shetlands-based counterpart to the extensive research arm housed in the Bear's Lair in Cincinnati and in UUI Kentucky. One of its primary missions is to support the US based Multiverse Project. It has a small staff directed remotely by Howard Watt and his associate Marlin the Dolphin.

At the moment, Colonel Where, Frau Schuylkill, Bruce Wallaroo, Octavius and I were there, standing by in a sparsely furnished room awaiting an arrival. An alarm sounded and Otto and the Bonobo Byzantia landed none too gracefully on a padded platform. Otto had one paw on the ape and one on his laptop containing a copy of Ursula 12. A blue identity badge hung around his neck. Byzz was dressed in a blue jumpsuit and wore a similar badge. Both looked bleary eyed. Once again, goofy Otto had accomplished his mission.

The Colonel and Frau walked over to give the space travelers an assist. The Otter released Byzz as he struggled to stand. She looked around somewhat frantically, shook off the paws extended toward her and backed away. "Leave me alone. You're kidnappers. I want the police. Send me back to Gaea!"

Bruce walked over to her and said, "Well, my hysterical Sheila, I am the Police. Chief Inspector Bruce Wallaroo currently of Interpol and you are an escaped criminal."

"I'm nothing of the sort. You have no proof of any crimes and I wasn't apprehended. I haven't escaped.

"Oh yes, you have. You've been charged in absentia. A bit out of the ordinary but valid, nonetheless. You're accused of aiding and abetting Caleb Cassowary's criminal extortion spree."

"I did no such thing. Caleb thought that up and executed it on his own."

Octavius intervened, "Come now, Ms. Bonobo. We're not here to argue your case. We want to make you a deal."

"Your Otter stooge here mentioned that. I'm not going to help bring in Caleb. I value my own life too much. He'd kick me to death. You don't know him."

Bruce laughed, "Oh yes we do. I had a real snootful of him when he was in Australia and these folks have all dealt with him ad nauseam. He's a dangerous nut."

"Exactly, and I don't want any part of him."

I spoke up, "Why don't you listen to what we have to offer, think about it and give us your answer in calmer circumstances. We have a few incentives you might want to consider."

She shook her head, sat on the floor and looked away.

Octavius laughed. "I'll take that as a maybe. We'll talk later. Meanwhile, we're going to escort you to a locked and guarded high level room in the hotel. It overlooks the ocean. Even if you have ape-like climbing abilities, I wouldn't think of trying to escape out the balcony. Sheer walls, rocks and high waves. Don't try to quantum transit, either. Howard can track you and we can bring you back. Frau Schuylkill will get you a meal. Tell her what you want to eat. Bruce and I will be by later along with FBI Special Agent Honey Badger on a Zoom connection. We'll also bring in Senhor L. Condor. He's the new Hexagon CTO. He may have a few thoughts about the Ursula project to explore with you. So long for now."

They left her shaking both in fear and rage.

Chapter Seventeen

Caleb launches a fierce cosmic coup.
With the Biosphere X vengeful crew.
He's the Chancellor now.
That means trouble and how.
He's distilling a troublesome brew.

Caleb was at his diabolical best. These birds on Biosphere X *(Home World, Ha!)* were boiling over with anger and desire for revenge on Earth, especially General Turmoil and Octavius Bear. Two of Caleb's favorites. Well, the Cassowary would give them the means to blow off that steam, kill off his adversaries and initiate his first steps toward cosmic conquest.

He needed a base, an army of followers and the wherewithal to procure enough technology to stage a major cyber war. Biosphere X wasn't ideal but it would do for starters. Gaea would be next and then he had lined up a series of planetary targets just waiting for his despotic guidance. The galaxy would be his.

It was a shame he was not a Quantum Motion Adept but he had the small portable transit device tucked under his diminutive wing. Some of these Home World birds were Adepts. Not the Protector or members of the Council but several members of the military. He must coopt them as soon as possible. Meanwhile, he had a little more work to do on the Protector. He returned to the Throne Aerie for another audience.

The Protector welcomed him but as usual, given his inherent paranoia, was somewhat reticent in dealing with this ominous bird. He had not seen such an intense and excitable avian in his long life. A vulture himself, he understood the predatory rules and techniques of conquest but had not developed the passion for dominance that this fellow exhibited. He was a true believer in the inevitable triumph of the successors to the dinosaurs and like the Protector was utterly convinced of the bird's total superiority over all other species. He would let him speak.

Caleb was nothing if not diffident. "Greetings, Most High! Thank you for allowing me into your presence again. I am honored."

The Protector flapped a wing. "You have my interest, Cassowary. Do not abuse it."

"I shall not, Sire. Am I correct in assuming we agree on what should be the rightful place of avians in the cosmic order?"

"Yes, yes, we are superior, actually supreme, but I am at a loss as to the best way to enforce that on the rest of our planetary neighbors. Physical attacks are troublesome, expensive and uncertain."

"Not just your neighbors, Majesty, the galaxy and cosmos."

"Such ambition. I will admit that you have vision, Cassowary but how would you turn that vision into fact?"

"I have a detailed plan, Most High, but I lack the authority to implement it. Perhaps as your Chancellor, I might. I note you do not have one."

"For good reason. No one is qualified. Convince me that you are."

"You are correct that physical wars can be wasteful and dangerous. Witness your conflict with that abominable horse, General Turmoil."

"You are not to mention his name in my presence."

"But wouldn't you like to wreak vengeance on him and his cronies? And what about that arrogant Kodiak Bear, Octavius?"

"Of course, but I am not prepared to sustain the sort of loss we suffered the last time. Does your detailed plan deal with them?"

"Indeed, Sire, and with no danger to the Home World. The secret is Computing and Telecommunications Technology. Forgive my immodesty, but I am a technological genius second to none. With appropriate resources at my disposal, I will permanently cripple Earth through a progression of disasters that will include those two criminals. They need never even know Biosphere X was involved. Then, further triumphs."

"Very well, you may proceed but keep me informed. I shall apprise the Council of my decision and alert the military. I am depending on you, Lord Chancellor."

Chapter Eighteen

The film is proceeding apace,
And it's time for the usual chase.
It's not really the same.
Since this time it's on Flame.
But the engine is up for the race.

Hooray for Hollywood! Well, not really. "Ура для Moskva!" Preston Pavel Polar Productions were typically housed in studios outside of Russia's capital city. Right now, there were several crews in remote locations, shooting and editing the footage for his latest extravaganza. He had decided to call it The Cyber Chaos Caper. Ouch! Too close for comfort.

He was currently ensconced in a large Polar Paradise conference room converted into a science fiction headquarters. His assistant, Bree, in an abbreviated secretarial costume was seated at an elaborate communications panel pressing buttons and trying to look like she knew what she was doing. Suddenly the door burst open and two tough looking wildcats, *(local Scots talent)* brandishing very serious looking weapons raced into the room, grabbed her and dragged her out, screaming as she went. One of them fired a laser blast at Preston and shouted. "Don't try to follow us. She'll get it if you do. Polar, lay off this Cyber Chaos Case or you'll never see your assistant alive again." He fired a second time for good measure.

Preston smiled. "OK Cut!" He looked at the cinematographer. "I think that was a good one. We'll check it in the rushes." The Lynx nodded.

Bree came back into the room, adjusting her costume as she did. "Preston, tell them not to be so rough. I bruise very easily." He ignored her. He turned to the production assistants. "What's next?"

"A chase scene in the fire engine. We're set up in the courtyard. You race out the door, over the drawbridge and into the truck, Lord David *(who was playing Preston's butler)* is driving. You follow the wildcat's car with the screaming Bree out of the parking lot at a breakneck pace with the siren howling and bell ringing."

"We'll do the rest of the chase scenes with CGI graphics later. Unfortunately, they get away. So you have to invade the Hexagon and get her back, killing off the terrorist in the process. The Hex is nearby in our film."

"When do we go to the Hexagon? It's really in Kentucky, isn't it?"

The German Shepherd replied. "This weekend. The Bearoness is loaning us her SST. Wait till you see this place. It's huge and state of the art. We can photograph the exterior to our heart's content. A lot of the interior is restricted. A Condor is in charge. I think you know him."

"If it's who I think it is, he was in my last film. By the way, does the terrorist have a name?"

"We have a few candidates. It's up to you to pick one. Claus, Cadmus, Caesar, Carl, Carew."

"Let's go with Claus. He's a Cassowary, isn't he?"

"Ja, we brought two of them up from Australia. One of them is a part time actor. They both look very scary."

"OK. Claus Cassowary it is. Let's get down to the parking lot. I want to ride in that fire truck. Flame! Good name!"

An assembly of tourists was milling around waiting for the matinee idol to appear. "Is he coming down?"

"One of the grips replied, "Yeah this is his next scene."

The cinematographer shouted, "Action!" The hotel doors flew open and the two toughs rushed out, dragging Bree unceremoniously between them. She was screaming pathetically. They raced for a car that was idling at the parking lot entrance.

The doors slammed open again and Preston, brandishing a light saber and dressed in futuristic garb befitting a heroic Polar Bear, raced out and shouted "Quick. Simpkins, follow that car."

The fire engine sprang to life with a throaty roar, siren blaring as Preston leaped onto the running board. Off they went to the applause of the thrilled onlookers.

The chase was on.

Chapter Nineteen

The Great Bear calls a longstanding foe.
He thinks General Turmoil should know
That the Homeworld is back.
They may stage an attack.
His assault wasn't quite a death blow.

(Polar Paradise)

Octavius was seated in the Bearonial suite in front of a large computer screen. By his paw was the perpetual cask of mead. Belinda was ensconced on a luxurious chaise longue, champagne bowl in paw, chatting on a laptop with Ursula 12. I was seated near the Great Bear's desk watching as his huge paws manipulated an oversize keyboard and trackball.

"How do I get on Zoom, Maury?"

"Very easy! Who do you want to contact?"

"General Turmoil!"

I looked up in surprise. Those two seldom communicated and when they did it was usually not on the friendliest of terms. Belinda stopped in mid-sentence and swung her attention to her spouse.

"That's unusual, Tavi. What's prompting your call?"

"We believe Caleb is on Biosphere X. Given the Crazy Horse's history with that planet, I think he should be aware."

"OK" I said, "this connection is going to take a little work, The Business doesn't make it easy to reach the General."

After establishing a transatlantic hookup, I went through an endless series of transfers, inquiries and intercepts and being told the General was not available. The Bear interrupted, "This is Octavius Bear. It's important that I speak to him <u>now</u>."

The underling on the other end of the line loudly sucked in his breath and said, "Please hold, Doctor Bear, I will try to reach him."

(Hold music. Octavius hated hold music. So do I.)

Finally, a horse voice whickered over the speaker. "Turmoil!"

"Hello General, this is Octavius Bear. Are you set up for a session on Zoom?"

"Hello Bear, I can be. Just a minute. I must say this call is something of a surprise. Smedley. Set this up on Zoom."

Octavius nodded to me and I did a bit of digital dancing on the keyboard. The screen switched and a black equine face appeared. "Can you see me?"

"Yes, how about this end?"

"Loud, clear and visual. What's up?"

"We're not certain but we may be in for a little excitement from our bird friends on Biosphere X."

"I wondered how long it would take. I guess they've reestablished their hierarchy. I doubt if their infrastructure is back. Or their military. We did a number on them. What makes you think we'll hear from them."

"We believe Caleb Cassowary is there."

"The Fugitive Technologist. How did you ever let him get away? He's on Home World? Our people thought he was on Gaea."

"He was but we are reasonably sure he skipped to the Home World. We have his former assistant in custody here in the Shetlands. We brought her back from Gaea. We're trying to persuade her to cooperate with us in bringing Caleb in. So far she's non-committal."

"Send her to us. We'll get her lined up."

"We're still in the carrot phase. I'll let you know if and when we need a stick."

"Wherever that damned Cassowary pops up, trouble walks in. Any thoughts on what those crazies might do?"

"After the shellacking you gave them, I doubt if they'll stage an overt physical attack. I think they're still licking their wounds from the last one. I bet Superbird may be cooking up some kind of cyberattack although I don't know how sophisticated Biosphere X's technology is. They seem to have a bruit force mentality."

"Let's not underestimate them especially when Caleb's there. We need to take him out before he stirs things up."

"We're working on that. If we need your help, we'll call."

"I think you're right about them going cyber if they go at all. Those birds are paranoid. Trust doesn't come easy for them. He may have an uphill climb to get them to buy his act, whatever it is."

"He staged a pretty destructive show here carrying out his extortion. We're still cleaning up the mess. I want to cut him off at the pass before he gets active. Thank goodness his ego keeps tripping him up."

"OK, we'll increase our surveillance on Home World. You and I don't cooperate often but this time, I think we need to. Thanks for the 'heads up.' Let us know if you have any luck with Ms. What's Her Name?"

"Byzantia, Byzz for short. She's a Bonobo. A brilliant Bonobo. Right now she's being a bit stubborn. I'm on my way for another round of negotiation. We'll see what happens."

"Good luck!" He cut the connection.

"OK Maury" said the Bear, "let's bring our primate prisoner in here. Ask the Colonel and Bruce to fetch her. And let's set up a Zoom session with Condo and Agent Badger. I think we're still in their active work hours. Although, I think Condo goes for 24 hours."

"It's persuasion time. Why don't you sit in, Bel? Having another female besides the FBI gal may help soften things up. I'd ask the Frau but it might look like we're piling on."

"Belinda chuckled, "Well, aren't we?"

Chapter Twenty

Our brave Otto has once more returned
And he's downing a drink that he earned.
But the jury's still out.
The whole group is in doubt.
Can Byzantia's head yet be turned?

(The Lion and Unicorn Lounge)

Dinner was fast approaching and the lounge denizens were indulging in the pre-prandial quaffs of their choice. A number of tourists had taken up seats and the few Octavians on paw were off in a corner.

"Where is everybody?" asked Chita.

"Why, Señorita Catt, I am here."

"Still trying, Jack? Sorry, No comprende! Or something like that. Seriously. Otto. What is going on? I understand you took a little Multiverse trip today."

"Shh, Chita. Keep your voice down. Multiverse is still a secret like the Ursulas. Yes, I did. I brought back a guest."

"Who?"

"Byzantia Bonobo."

It was Dancing Dan's turn. "Who?"

"She was Caleb Cassowary's assistant and designer of the Ursulas. The two of them skipped town courtesy of quantum motion after their extortion plot blew up in their faces. She was on Gaea. We don't know where he is. Octavius is right now trying to find out."

Lord David smiled, "Twisting her arm?"

"No, making her an offer she can't refuse."

The Frau laughed. "At nine feet tall and 1400 pounds, Herr Bear can be quite persuasive."

Otto chuckled, "So can the Police and Condo."

"Why Condo?"

"He'd like to have her back at the Hexagon to work on Ursula 13. Provided he can trust her. Isn't that right, Ursie?"

The AGI had been lying quietly in her laptop on one of the cocktail tables.

"That's correct, Otto. She was our top designer. I'm still quite effective but the series could use upgrades. New tech! More capacity! Faster speeds! More complex algorithms. More sophisticated intelligence."

"More intelligent than you? You're kidding!"

"No, Chita. We have to keep growing. She was very important to us. I miss her. I don't miss Caleb."

Otto laughed, "Nobody does but we have to find him and shut him down."

"Any idea where he might be?"

"The smart money says he's on Biosphere X."

The Frau snorted, "Those verdammt birds. We ought to blow the whole planet up."

Lord David shook his spotted head. "I'd never heard of them before I got here. They sound like a pretty dangerous bunch."

Otto agreed, "They are! They're convinced that avians are destined to rule the universe."

"Well, that's not too uncommon. There are a lot of folks who believe in their own supremacy. I ran into them all the time when I was still a member of the Dalmatian Court."

Dan spoke up. "But this combination with Caleb Cassowary sounds like it's really incendiary."

"You got it, Dan."

"Anything we can do to help?"

"Can you drive a fire engine to another planet?"

Chapter Twenty One

The cast and the crew hit the air
On the fabulous, swift Aquabear.
Then it's on to the Hex.
That exciting complex.
First, a stopover at the Bear's Lair.

The film crew clambered off the shuttle helicopter and walked across to the Concorde SST at Abeardeen Airport lugging and dragging cameras, sound equipment, drones and lighting. They broke into two groups. One was going to film the takeoff of the sleek bird that was going to take Preston and his team from the Shetlands to Kentucky where he would encounter Claus Cassowary, the Cyber Terrorist. Belinda had assigned the Flying Tigers to transport the matinee idol and his associates to the Bear's Lair in Cincinnati and then arranged transit over to the Hexagon in the Kentucky hills.

His other team boarded the ship after stowing all of their gear in the cargo hold. They were greatly impressed. The fuselage was narrow but the seats were luxurious and an amply stocked galley beckoned from the rear.

The speakers crackled. A feline voice. "Welcome aboard the Aquabear, Ladies and Gentlebeasts. I am Captain Benedict Tigris. My co-pilot today is Galatea Tigris. This is the last flying Concorde in existence. The prize possession of our employer, the Bearoness Belinda Bearnaise Bruin Bear nee Black. We are happy to have you with us."

"Shortly after takeoff we will fly over the Atlantic Ocean at supersonic speed on our way to the North American continent. Once in American air space we will reduce our speed to subsonic as required by law and proceed to the Lair of Octavius Bear in Cincinnati. There you will be met by members of the Great Bear's household and your trip to the UUI Hexagon will be facilitated."

"Please be seated, adjust your seat belts and prepare for takeoff. Once we are airborne, we will be by in the cabin to answer your questions and provide drinks and amenities. Thank you."

The jet engines set up a scream and the Concorde moved out to the Abeardeen taxiway on the way to the runway and the Atlantic sky. On the ground, the second unit was photographing Preston Polar's progress in getting airborne. They weren't sure why. Some future film? The SST raised its 'droop snoot', roared and leaped into the air. On to the Hexagon and the 'terrorists'.

Attaining supersonic speed is a bit of a non-event. Only the Mach meter over the cockpit door indicates that the sound barrier has been breached. The team was out of their seats and clustering around Preston who was giving instructions on the next day's shoot at the UUI Hexagon.

Herr Gustav Schäferhund was sitting next to Preston. The crew called him 'Hund'. He was outlining the day's schedule with the Polar interrupting frequently. "We have hired two Cassowaries from Australia. One is a part time actor. He will be our villain. The other is on standby. The Raccoon Brothers have sent a script on to them. He is to act like a mad scientist."

Preston picked it up. "When we arrive at the Hexagon, you will be floored by the place. It's huge, super modern and scientific to the hilt. I want the drones to take in everything – the building; the antennas; the helipad; the wind turbines; the surrounding landscape; even the parking lots."

"The real Hexagon is in Kentucky. Ours will be in Scotland not that far from the Polar Paradise castle. It will be called Cyber Complex. We may or may not use the SST footage we shot at the airport but it's good to have just in case."

Back to the Hund. "I think you all know the original Chief Technical Officer at the Hex as it's called was a rogue Cassowary. Our villain is based on him. He shut down all the technical resources run by UUI and was holding them for extortion. Our friend Octavius Bear foiled him. I'm not sure how."

"The new CTO is a Condor we have used in the past. He had a part in the Laughing Laird. I've had a Zoom conference with him. He is unwilling to appear in the film but has given us permission to make some restricted interior shots of the complex and is letting us use a conference facility as Claus' office. That's where the duel will take place. Later we will develop CGI sequences to show the Cyber War technology he plans to use on the world. Claus is the original Dirty Bird."

"In our script, Preston catches Claus before he gets a chance to put his plan in play. Lightsaber fight! Claus is wounded and then Preston rescues Bree. He turns the Cassowary over to the Police. The film ends with the two of them aboard the fire engine Flame driving off into the sunset and Bearmoral Castle."

The film crew was used to Preston's derring-do and were ready to conjure up another flight of fantasy although this time it would be in futuristic dress and surroundings. Preston still wears a cape. All super heroes do. But he's traded in his sword for a lightsaber. Sydney and Sheldon Raccoon were ready at a moment's notice to create 21st century swashbuckling *(not sure what that means)* action and dialogue on call as Preston got another one of his off-the-wall brilliant ideas.

The Hund was then on the hook to produce the end result. The two Grizzly Production assistants, Doris and Ella got to do the nitty gritty. However, this time, each one of them had a small part in this extravaganza. They were finally getting some screen exposure.

Bree had been sitting in her luxurious aircraft seat munching on snacks from the well-stocked galley and wondering what new preposterous stunts she would be called upon to execute. Not much in the brain department but plucky.

The discussions ended when the co-pilot got on the intercom and said, "Ladies and Gentlebeasts, we are now entering Cincinnati Air Traffic Control. We will soon be making our final approach for the Bear's Lair. Please return to your seats and secure all materials which you have taken out. Make sure your seats are upright and your tray tables are in the stowed position. We will be on the ground shortly."

The grinding sound of descending flaps coupled with a change in the key of the engines' sound announced their descent onto the runway cleverly disguised as an Interstate Highway extension complete with phony construction equipment. The landing gear thumped on the thick concrete and the SST's 'droop snoot' lowered to provide unimpeded visibility while taxiing. Another routine trans-Atlantic trip had come to a successful close.

They rolled up to a large Romanesque hangar, rotated on the apron and shut the engines down. The ground crew arrived with airstairs as the passenger doors were opened. Other service personnel were already at the cargo hold and began unloading the baggage and gingerly handling the movie equipment.

Two individuals came out to meet the passengers. "Good afternoon everyone" said a Porcupine. "My name is Howard Watt, Science Officer for Octavius Bear and this Gentledog is our Butler, Huntley Husky. Welcome!"

Preston, Hund, Bree, the Raccoons, Lukas and the film crew entered the Bear's Lair mansion. Awed by the size and opulence, they proceeded to the rooms assigned to them and then to the lounge where generous libations awaited them. Dinner would be forthcoming shortly.

Later, even world-weary Preston was impressed by the hospitality afforded them. "Tell me, Huntley, is this treatment an everyday event when the Bear and his entourage are in residence?"

"Oh yes sir, we all live very comfortably here at the Bear's Lair. What may I get for you? Another drink? Was dinner sufficient? Are your rooms adequate?"

Bree chirped, "Everything is lovely, including you, Mr. Huntley."

If he could, the Husky would have blushed. The young sow was an obvious flirt. He ignored the compliment.

Howard had joined them. "We'll be off early in the morning. It's almost an hour's drive to the Hexagon. I've laid on two vans for your use. I'll accompany you. Have a good evening."

*****

Fortunately, it was a practically cloudless morning, ideal for exterior shots of the huge edifice. As the two vans climbed the shallow hill leading to the Hex, a sharp intake of breath was the common reaction. This place was spectacular. Octavius Bear had once again outdone himself. The cinematographer and his crew piled out in the parking lot and got the drones ready to go on their aerial missions, recording the copper colored giant and its surroundings.

Howard led Preston, Gustav, Bree and the two PAs up to the Hex entrance. Sitting in the reception hall were two Cassowaries, Oliver and Noah.

Oliver was the part time actor and would play Claus. Noah would be the standby and do some of the expected stunts. Greetings all around.

Howard was leading them to the elevators that would take them to the fourth floor and Condo's offices. As they moved along, Bree was staring in awe and Preston was furiously making notes on his iPad and firing instructions at Doris and Ella.

The Hund was explaining the scenarios to the two Cassowaries. They didn't notice the curious and fearful stares they were evoking as they passed staff members in the hall. When they reached the top floor and the open work spaces, the looks were even more intense. Howard chuckled to himself. He'd have to alert Condo.

They reached his office, filed in and were greeted by the newly appointed CTO. Paw and wing shakes all around. A large laptop on Condo's desk housed a copy of Ursula 12 who was in passive mode, recording all that was going on but not revealing her presence. Ursulas were a secret known to the Octavians and a limited number of Advanced Super Computing Center staff responsible for their development. Byzz had led the group. Where was she now?

Howard went over to Condo and whispered in his ear. He laughed, shook his head and went back to his desk. A moment later his face appeared on a large screen. He spoke: "Attention all personnel, this is CTO L. Condor speaking. For your information we have a film team here at the Hexagon for the next two days photographing a cinema feature starring the famous Preston Pavel Polar. *(Preston walked around the desk and peered over Condo's shoulder, waving at the camera. There was a smattering of applause in some quarters.)* We are delighted to welcome him. They will be operating in assigned areas and there will be minimum disturbance of your activities."

(He gestured to the two Cassowaries to join him.) "These two gentlebirds are Noah and Oliver Cassowary. They are actors from Australia who will be appearing in the film. I assure you that Caleb has not returned. None of you need be concerned. I have been informed that neither of these birds are related to or know our former CTO. Please return to your normal pursuits. Thank you."

The screen went blank and the condor winked at Howard. He turned to Preston. "Octavius asked us to give you full cooperation. Let us know how we can help. Please follow me to the rooms we have set aside for your use."

The film crew and actors were puzzled by Condo's remarks. They had a vague knowledge of who Caleb Cassowary was and his attempts at shutting down UUI and much of the world's computing and telecommunications power. Their film would be derived in part from that story.

But they had no idea of his escape with Byzantia to an alternate universe and no one was going to enlighten them. As far as the world at large was concerned, the two fugitives were hidden away somewhere on Earth. There would be no mention in the movie of Multiverse activity since no one was aware of it. Preston's flights of fancy did not encompass space travel. Octavius, Howard and Condo wanted it to stay that way.

They entered into the conference room, which was set up with surrealistic, non-functioning devices; subdued lighting; control consoles and large screens. *(Actually this would have delighted Caleb.)* Bree was led off to a small cubicle where she was being held prisoner by the madbird Claus. Oliver was given a sidearm and headset which he strapped on as he seated himself in front of an imposing and completely useless console. *(Correction: It had a myriad of flashing lights and buttons.)* Noah was similarly attired.

Lukas Lynx, the cinematographer, had arrived from supervising the drone flights and was positioning the cameras and sound units. Doris handed the Cassowaries their scripts which they had already absorbed. Preston was poised outside the door, lightsaber at the ready, prepared to come crashing in and attacking Claus. Stand-in Noah would take most of the brunt of the fight.

The Hund was doing last minute checks. He nodded at Lukas. "Lights, Sound, Camera, Action!" Another cinematic triumph was in progress.

Chapter Twenty Two

Caleb bullies his way to the top.
And as Chancellor, sets up his shop.
He's insulting and crass
To the top Army brass.
Will his arrogant ploys ever stop?

(Biosphere X)

'Chancellor' Caleb strutted out of the throne room with a smug grin on his misshapen face. Things were progressing. He now must trigger the first stages of his elaborate plan of conquest.

He had gotten from the Protector what amounted to a Home World version of a free rein. He debated whether to try and overthrow that Vulture or operate from the more flexible position of Chancellor. Did he want to rule from Biosphere X? Probably not! Thoughts for the future.

Right now, he needed to produce a few results. First step, the military garrison and the Generalissimo in Charge – as expected, a Ferruginous Hawk. (*Buteo regalis*) Caleb wondered what had happened to the Eagles. They seemed to be in short supply. Something to do with the Earth attack? Oh, well!

As he strode across the fields surrounding the military headquarters, he observed an array of soldier birds performing close order drill with weapons that looked 50 years old or more. To his left was a rifle range. More of the same. He half expected to come upon a couple of long ago vintage tanks. He looked in vain for telecommunication antennas or any other signs of 21st century technology. If they existed, they were well hidden. There was a small airfield with hangars housing a few large transport jet aircraft. Where were the fighters and air defense planes? Sure, Birds could fly but not supersonically. No rocketry in sight. At least Gaea could launch satellites.

He approached the citadel housing the garrison, offices and utility rooms of the top military brass.

Using his extraordinary size and tree-like legs to impress the armed guards who occupied the entrance to the stronghold, he peremptorily ordered, "Tell the Generalissimo that Chancellor Cassowary is here to see him."

The guards didn't know who this unusual bird was but they were sure there was no such thing as a Chancellor in the Home World government. "I'm sorry, sir, but we can't grant you admittance."

Caleb stared at him with his hypnotic yellow eyes and said, "I suggest you call the General's office before I kick you across this lobby."

One guard raised his weapon but another took up a phone and dialed through. "This is Lobby Security. There is an unusual individual here who claims he is the Protector's Chancellor and wishes to see the Generalissimo."

The Protector's announcement of Caleb's appointment had just reached the military headquarters. The Adjutant on the other end of the line told the guard that he would come down and meet the Chancellor. "Is he alone?"

"Yes sir. I'll tell him you're coming."

"Colonel Goshawk will be down shortly, sir."

Caleb laughed internally. Nothing like a little bullying to inspire your inferiors. Meantime, he perused the guards' weapons. Primitive but no doubt, still effective at short range. Of course, security duty did not require state of the art ordnance. One thing he needed to learn from the Generalissimo is the level of preparedness of the armed forces. How adequate was their technological weaponry? Does Cyber War mean anything to them?

As he looked around at the military memorabilia that adorned the lobby, he couldn't help thinking there was more form than function here. He would deal with that.

A brown goshawk with elaborate epaulettes attached to his wings entered the area from a large, glass enclosed door.

"Lord Chancellor, Welcome. I am Colonel Goshawk, adjutant to the Generalissimo. He is awaiting you."

"Well, let's not waste any more of your or my valuable time. Take me to him."

"The Colonel cocked his head but said nothing. His thoughts ran along the lines of 'pompous jerk.' He nodded to the guards who sprang to open the ornate door. The Colonel hopped ahead. Caleb strode through.

"Tell me, Colonel, have you ever seen duty on Earth?"

"Only briefly, in disguise, sir. Not one of my finest experiences."

"On Earth, Brown goshawks are from Australia. So am I, originally. Not one of my finest experiences, either. Are your descendants Australian?"

"I don't really know, Milord. I am an orphan."

And a dullard, thought the Cassowary. They went down a long corridor bedecked with regimental flags. Caleb was unimpressed. The adjutant knocked on an ostentatious door with his retracted claws.

A harsh avian voice shrieked, "Come!" The goshawk opened the door and stood aside. A grey Ferruginous Hawk sat perched behind an ornate and uncluttered desk. "Lord Chancellor, welcome. I am Generalissimo Hawk."

"Let's cut through the social small talk, Hawk. We're both busy birds. I don't know what the Protector told you members of the military but my primary remit is to ensure that Home World is once again prepared for cosmic conquest."

This hit the Generalissimo between his piercing eyes. "Cosmic Conquest. Not sure I understand."

"No, you wouldn't. For all of the Protector's and Council's crowing, Biosphere X is a military backwater. This planet is second rate or worse."

The officer was enraged. "Now, just a second, Lord Chancellor. That is neither true nor correct. We serve the Home World bravely and very well."

"And lose dramatically to Earthbound Horses. I'm surprised you still have your job."

"We were victims of a sneak attack."

"That you didn't see coming. With an appropriate early warning system and defensive equipment, that disaster needn't have happened. Let me ask you a few questions: What is the military's technology level?"

"I don't know how to answer that precisely. We have computers, naturally, and laser guided weaponry. Our communication systems are relatively new. We have internet style access. Our satellites are few. Our GPS system is restricted to military use only. The Council will not finance more than two rocket launch facilities. On the other side of the planet. We have a few supersonic and cargo aircraft but as you can imagine, being avian, most of our flights are individual. I notice that you are flightless."

That last remark didn't go over well. Caleb frowned. "You sound like you are well positioned...for the 1980's. What about your cyber warfare capability? Offensive and defensive? Do you have a department dedicated to Cyber War? Can you undermine an enemy's infrastructure; destroy their financial, health; government; education; transportation; supply chain; information and social media abilities? Can you cripple their military's ability to function? Can you defend against similar attacks from other planets? How many computer and communications specialists do you employ?"

"You can't answer those questions satisfactorily, can you? Well, I will see to it that the Biosphere's defense system advances into the 21st century rapidly, starting today. Good day, Generalissimo. Go back to your heraldry."

He stalked out of the office and headed back to the Protector's Aerie. The Generalissimo stared in shock. Finally, he shouted, "Colonel Hawk. Get in here. Who the hell is that arrogant bird? Find out!"

The Protector was meeting with the Council when the Chancellor stormed in. Ignoring protests, he interrupted the proceedings. "Do you gentlebirds have any idea how utterly obsolete your military really is. They couldn't do battle with an asteroid of mice much less a fully up to date planet. You must be prepared to take strong steps and make major investments to upgrade their abilities immediately. Cosmic conquest can be yours and vengeance can be wreaked on your enemies but only if you take tough and robust measures. The Generalissimo has to go. Probably many of his officers as well."

Several of the Council tried to speak but he rode right over them. "When I arrived here, I had expected to find a vigorous, well equipped, highly motivated army, air force and navy. I see none of that. You lack the first basic fundamentals of waging cyber war and cyber terrorism. Those are today's means of domination, not a bunch of parading recruits. Where are your technologists? Where is your technology?"

Once more the members of the Council tried to regain the floor. Caleb was having none of it. One, a young Falcon named Peregrine was nodding his head in approval. Caleb continued. "Lord Protector, in order to set up an adequate base for Biosphere X development, I need an environment where modern technical skills are available and equipment is at claw."

"As you know, I came recently from Gaea. I'm going to return there temporarily to initiate a series of programs which I will then transfer to Home World. I will leave a list of actions which must be carried out here immediately. I assume you will give that responsibility to a Council member. Let me know who. Perhaps this Peregrine here. I will return shortly. Good Bye."

He stalked out. He would go back to his quarters and then with the help of the Quantum Motion device, he would leave for Gaea where he was sure Byzz would be waiting for him, ready to do his bidding. It's a pity she lacks his ambition. She is brilliant but reluctant to engage fully in the warfare that his cosmic plans called for. Fortunately, she can be easily persuaded and replaced.

This time on Gaea, all he needed was some equipment. She had access to the space suit and weapons he would require. Where he was going lacked an atmosphere. A space suit and oxygen supply was critical. Byzz would provide them, He called her and told her of his imminent arrival on Gaea and his requirements. Little did he know where Byzantia was at the moment.

Chapter Twenty Three

The big picture's completed and now
It was time for the crew to say "ciao."
Preston conquered once more.
He could head for the door
With another true cinema "Wow."

(Maury here)

Back on Earth, the film was wrapping up. The Cassowary Cyber Terrorist was defeated and jailed. Bree was free. Preston had once again saved the day. The Hexagon was occupied by the good guys and Earth was no longer under serious threat. At least for the moment.

Now if the same thing only applied to reality. No such luck. Caleb was still a formidable adversary, even if he was a Multiverse away. We needed to deal with him.

During the shoots, Preston had been making a pest of himself trying to get as much information about Caleb as possible. Verisimilitude in film making. We fed him a lot of stuff about the Cassowary prior to his extortion attempt but nothing since.

The script writers, not lacking in imagination, had filled in a lot of gaps. The screen Caleb was definitely a Raccoon Brothers and Schäferhund creature, looking even more threatening than the original. Little did they know how close they had come to the real thing. They had all returned to Polar Paradise. The Cassowaries were on their way back to Australia.

The Lion and Unicorn were rejoicing on their potential upswing in business and the long lasting publicity they would get from the film when it was released. They had hammed up their famous fight which the crew faithfully recorded for posterity. They also placed orders for a substantial increase in their inventory. They finished discussions with Belinda and reached agreement on expanding the Lion and Unicorn Lounge at Polar Paradise. Fiona was beside herself in delight. Her empire was growing. She'd have to make arrangements to use Dolly, Holly, Molly and Polly on a permanent basis. "Bark!"

Preston's lawyer, Sasha Sable, and I had entered into negotiations on financial considerations but then I turned it over to Wolford Wolverine, Octavius' counsellor and the Chief Legal Officer of UUI. He put the lawyerly touches on the transactions. Suffice it to say, Bel and Octavius would be the recipients of substantial sums which, if history were any guide, would end up in the paws of the Octavians. The previous films continued to rake in healthy residuals for our cast. As their agent, I got a piece of the action.

The Twins managed to get Preston to add his visage to the panoply of avatars they were installing in the new version of the Bold Brave Brilliant Bumptious Bears game. They were a bit put out that they did not have parts in this last extravaganza but the additions to the game were adequate compensation. Mlle Woof was greatly relieved at not having to follow them around across sets and sound stages.

Nobody was in any doubt that this one was going to be another Preston smasheroo. The magic was still there and the Polar Paradise / Hexagon combination was icing on the cake. The two Cassowary actors had added to their Down Under resumes.

Chita, Jack, Lord David and Dan had been pressed into action with small but juicy parts. Once again the Frau and Colonel abstained. Chita shimmied her way across the screen and stretched her sinuous legs as a femme fatale. Jack swaggered but was no competition for Preston. Davey and Dan drove the fire engine wildly in the chase scenes.

Even Flame got something. A new, louder siren.

Chapter Twenty Four

Ms. Byzantia's under duress.
She is stuck in a heck of a mess.
Extreme pressure is on
To say where Caleb's gone.
Will she finally give in and confess?

(The Bearonial Suite)

"Come in, Byzz. Make yourself comfortable." Octavius was at his gracious best. He was making sure Preston and his crew didn't know Byzz was at the hotel.

"I don't want to be comfortable. I don't want to be here."

"You've made that quite plain. However, you are here. You do realize you could be in serious trouble. Notice I said 'could.' Inspector Wallaroo here is ready to throw the time honored book at you and we will be connecting shortly with Special Agent Honey Badger of the FBI who also has a good pitching arm. In addition to all the other accusations against you, there's also an additional charge of illegal flight from prosecution. Pretty messy."

The Colonel chimed in. "We don't think you wanted to be part of Caleb's crazy scheme but you couldn't figure out a way to get out from under. He's a real and present threat. We want to put a stop to his nonsense and we want you to help us."

She bowed her head.

Octavius turned to me. "Maury, hook up with Agent Badger and Senhor Condor. Yes, Byzz. We're applying pressure but nowhere near what law enforcement will do if we back away. We're going to offer you an out. The FBI isn't too happy with the idea but they're willing to go along. Chief Inspector Wallaroo has had a few conversations with Interpol and they're willing to look the other way providing you work with us."

She looked over at Belinda who smiled. A Polar Bear smile is not always the most reassuring. Belinda's was.

The screen flashed and two faces appeared. Condo was sitting at the desk that once belonged to the Cassowary. He spread his immense wings momentarily by way of greeting. Byzz winced. She knew he would be good for the Hexagon and for technology in general. He would certainly get the Ursula 13 program off to a good start. She wanted to be part of it.

The Badger was all business. The white stripe down the center of her grey head led past two piercing eyes to a twitching snout. A threatening stare, no doubt practiced in front of a mirror to cause no end of discomfort to her victims. She announced herself. "Special Agent Badger." Byzz winced once again.

Octavius took up the discussion. "Byzantia, or would you prefer Ms. Bonobo?"

She shrugged.

"Byzantia, when you spoke to Otto, who isn't here by the way, you told him you were pretty sure Caleb went to Biosphere X. We can't track him. Our system only works for individuals leaving or entering Earth. We can track you now that you're here but someone transiting from Gaea to Home World won't appear on our screens."

"He's won't be on Biosphere X."

"What?"

"He's won't be on Biosphere X. He called me half an hour ago. He's going back to Gaea. He's working for the birds but the equipment and software he needs are on Gaea and of course, here on Earth. He wants me to join him. He thinks I'm still on Gaea. He said something about satellites. That's where I was working before your crazy otter snatched me away."

Shockwaves around the room and on the screens.

"He's not aware I hate his guts or he doesn't really care. He thinks I'll scamper right along to serve once again as his chump du jour."

The Bear looked at her. "That's what we'd like you to do. We want to capture him but first we want to know what the Home World crowd has in mind. Are they on the warpath again?"

Bruce nodded. "Get us that information and we'll drop the charges. What do you say, Agent Badger?"

"As long as we get him, I'll be satisfied. I want him in prison. And I'm not enthused about an attack by those psychotic avians, either. Sorry to tell you this, lady, but you're small potatoes in this case."

Condo, who had been listening to all of this attentively, said, "But she's not small potatoes to our Ursula program. Can we trust you enough to let you return to the Hex, Byzz? You could be a great asset but I don't want to be looking back over my wings every minute."

The Bonobo looked down and around the room. She got another smile from Belinda. Maybe the Polar Sow wasn't so bad after all. Byzz was clearly outnumbered but what they were offering was appealing. She didn't want to spend the rest of her life as a fugitive. She'd like to return to Earth but as a free agent. She ached to return to the Hexagon. The Ursula program was her first love. But she also wanted to avenge herself on Caleb and the thought of the birds of the Home World sent shivers down her spine.

She nodded her head. "OK, what exactly do you want me to do?"

Sighs of relief. Octavius smiled. *(That was scary. Millions of teeth.)* "Change of plan. We originally wanted you to just locate him for us so we could bring him in. We still want that. But now we want to know what the Biosphere X plan that he's working on is all about. The fact that he's back in Gaea makes it a bit easier. We can infiltrate there more easily. There's a sizeable mixture of species on Gaea and we won't stand out like we would in an all-bird world. I don't know how Otto managed it while he was there. I guess he spent half his time zapping away from his pursuers.. Can you go back easily? Do you think the Gaea Telecom Center knows you're missing?"

"I can cook up some kind of an excuse if I need one. I was sick after celebrating our last launch. Everyone will be busy. We have a couple of more space shots coming up shortly. Communications and space junk surveillance. I'll just slide back in. I won't look for Caleb. I don't want to seem eager. Let him find me. He's probably hiding. With his looks, he really sticks out."

"OK, let's get you fed, rested and ready to go. Tomorrow morning, back to Gaea!

Chapter Twenty Five

Caleb takes off for Gaea once more
He's determined to settle a score.
It will take all he's worth
To get even with Earth
And to kill off the Bear in this war.

Caleb returned to his quarters and created a list of actions he would require the Council to carry out over the next few weeks. It involved major expense and changes in staffing. New computing and telecommunications equipment; recruiting and intensive training for a select number of birds; software acquisition and installation; testing, testing, testing. He sent it to the Protector's office to be passed on to Peregrine, the young but upcoming Falcon Council member who had been selected to head up the program. Caleb would see him on his return from Gaea.

Gaea! He packed a small bag with his necessities, took up the portable transit device, clawed in the coordinates for the Gaea Telecommunications and Computing Center, hit the 'Go' button and plummeted, semi-conscious through space.

Quantum motion is something of a trial for Passives like Caleb. Unlike Adepts, they lack personal control and must rely on external guidance whether personal or technological, to reach their objective.

When they last arrived back on Gaea, after their escape from Earth, he and Byzz *(mostly Byzz)* had miniaturized the clunky quantum device he had originally stolen on his first trip to the planet. He could now tuck it under his foreshortened wing. He would need it as he carried out the first steps in his dastardly plan.

He would also need Byzz to support him one more time. She would, as usual, bow to his superior domination over her. Phase One required her assistance.

He would cripple Earth so they could not pursue him and then he would return to Biosphere X to launch his cyber raids of interstellar subjugation. Those birds would be his unwitting foils as he fashioned Cosmic Chaos. First

Earth, the Solar System, the exoplanets and the Milky Way and then intergalactic conquest. It was almost overwhelming in its ambitious ingenuity.

The quantum motion device beeped. He was approaching his target.

He landed in a field near the Center and spent the next few minutes recovering his equilibrium. As his mind cleared, lying there, he looked about. He remembered the landscape and the cluster of squat buildings that made up the complex. In the distance was the launch facility with another small rocket poised to go into trans-atmospheric space.

He would not approach the area. He was too unusual and easily recognized. As far as he knew, he was the only Southern Cassowary on Gaea, certainly here at the Center. That's why he needed Byzz. She would get him what he needed for his attack on Earth.

He checked his quantum device. Intact and functioning. Then he took up his phone and placed a call to the Bonobo.

"You have reached the phone of Byzantia Bonobo. I am not available at the moment. Please leave a message and I will return your call as soon as I can." Beep!

"Damn that ape! I told her to expect me. Why isn't she standing by?"

"Hello Caleb!"

Byzz was standing over him. She had a miniature laser gun in her bag. She could have killed him there and then but Octavius wanted information. Patience!

"Well, Byzz. You found me."

"Yes, I tracked your arrival. That quantum device _we_ fashioned works rather well, doesn't it?

"Yes, yes. Now that you're here, I have orders for you. As I told you, I need a space suit and a large, long distance laser weapon. I also need you to program the quantum device to reach a large satellite orbiting Earth.

"That's a tall order, Caleb. A space suit that fits you will be most unusual. I may have to innovate. The weapon should be easier to come by. Are you planning to destroy an Earth Satellite?

"I'm planning to destroy Earth *__from__* a Satellite. The Advanced Super Computing Center was heavily involved in enhancing and supporting the GPS system. I have the knowledge to destroy it. You will provide me with the wherewithal. My sabotage will immobilize Earth for months, maybe years. That will occupy them sufficiently to call off their search for me…and for you.

"What are you doing on Biosphere X?"

"Biosphere X is a technologically obsolete backwater but it serves my purpose. Their lust for vengeance on Earth, especially General Turmoil and Octavius Bear, plays right into my claws. Those paranoid birds are not yet ready to wage Cyber warfare but I will whip them into shape. No one will know where my attacks are coming from until it's too late. Gaea is next on my takeover list. Then on to the entire Galaxy. Cosmic Chaos."

"Now go! Get what I want. Quickly! I will be hidden in that storeroom over there."

Byzz shook her head. She took a moment to organize her thoughts as she walked back to the Q block at the Center. Should she call Octavius and tell him what Caleb was up to? She decided not to. They'd mount up a small task force and try to capture him. She didn't want him captured. He was clever enough to escape yet again. She wanted him dead. A plan formed in her brilliant mind.

First stop, the arsenal. Swipe a space-capable, portable laser weapon. Then cobble together a space suit that would fit that outsized bird and get one for herself. She was going to accompany Caleb into the void. She would return to Earth without him.

The Development of Civilization-Volume 14 Part 6

GPS – The Global Positioning System

(From "An Introduction to Faunapology" by Octavius Bear Ph.D.)

(Excerpted from GPS.gov - Official U.S. Government information about the Global Positioning System (GPS))

The Global Positioning System (GPS) is a U.S.-owned utility that provides users with positioning, navigation, and timing (PNT) services. This system consists of three segments: the space segment, the control segment, and the user segment. The U.S. Air Force develops, maintains, and operates the space and control segments.

Space Segment
The space segment consists of a nominal constellation of 24 operating satellites that transmit one-way signals that supply the current GPS satellite position and time.

Control Segment
The control segment consists of worldwide monitor and control stations that maintain the satellites in their proper orbits through occasional command maneuvers and adjust the satellite clocks. It tracks the GPS satellites, uploads updated navigational data, and maintains health and status of the satellite constellation.

User Segment
The user segment consists of the GPS receiver equipment, which receives the signals from the GPS satellites and uses the transmitted information to calculate the user's three-dimensional position and time. Its users are in the multi-millions.

GPS Services

GPS satellites provide service to civilian and military users. The civilian service is freely available to all users on a continuous, worldwide basis. The military service is available to U.S. and allied armed forces as well as approved Government agencies.

Augmentations
A variety of GPS augmentation systems and techniques are available to enhance system performance to meet specific user requirements. These improve signal availability, accuracy, and integrity, allowing even better performance than is possible using the basic GPS civilian service.

Performance
The outstanding performance of GPS over many years has earned the confidence of millions of civil users worldwide. It has proven its dependability in the past and promises to be of benefit to users, throughout the world, far into the future.

Modernization
The United States is committed to an extensive modernization program, including the implementation of a second and a third civil signal on GPS satellites. The second civil signal will improve the accuracy of the civilian service and support some safety-of-life applications. The third signal will further enhance civilian capability and is primarily designed for safety-of-life applications, such as aviation.

Security and Backup
GPS was initially conceived to aid navigation. However, globally synchronized time has emerged as a much more critical function of the system. GPS clocks keep cell towers synchronized so calls can be passed between them. Many power grids use the clocks in equipment that fine-tunes the flow of electrical current. The financial industry uses GPS-dependent timing systems to timestamp ATM, funds transfer, credit card, and high-speed stock transactions. Computer networks, digital TV and radio, Doppler radar weather reporting, seismic monitoring, air traffic control—all utilize GPS clocks.

The rapid development of technology is opening up Earth to an increasingly wide variety of rare but potentially destructive cosmic threats. GPS is vulnerable.

UUI Aerospace and our Advanced Super Computing Center cooperate with and support the US Air Force in this highly essential service. GPS is a crucial component in the maintenance and continued growth of Earth's civilization. We are engaged in developing security, backup and bypass systems to mitigate GPS failures whether accidental or deliberately induced.

Chapter Twenty Six

Two space-suited figures progress
With a purpose on which they obsess.
With destructive intent
Caleb makes his descent
Toward a satellite of GPS.

The Bonobo trudged toward the storeroom and Caleb, pulling a small storage cart behind her. In it were two spacesuits and an oversized laser weapon all covered over with a tarp. Surprisingly, none of the Gaea Center security staff had challenged her. There were always weird things going on in the Q block. Curiosity was low and protection was more than a little lax.

She had managed to find a very large spacesuit designed for a bear. Ironic! She wouldn't tell Caleb. He'd have a fit. *(no pun)* He should be able to squeeze his ungainly frame into it. The helmet was big enough to accommodate his head, bony casque and double wattles.

The laser weapon was used to displace rocks and other detritus on asteroids. It had a long range and a powerful blast. Just what he wanted. The other suit was for her. She had her laser pistol tucked in one of its many utility pockets.

This was going to be a short trip. One way for the Cassowary. A route diversion for her. She rapped on the door of the storeroom and shouted. "Caleb, Open Up!"

Sounds of heavy legs stomping toward the portal. Locks clicking open. Two yellow eyes peered out at her. "Quiet, you fool. Do you want Security on our necks? Have you brought what I need?"

"It's all here. Try the suit on."

He reached into the cart and pulled out her small suit. "Is this a joke. Do you expect me to fit into this tiny thing?"

"No, that's for me. I'm going with you. Your suit is on the bottom under the weapon."

"You're going with me? Why?

"After you've done your number on Earth's GPS system, they'll be searching for both of us. I'm leaving Gaea. We can travel together or we can split up after the big blast. I don't like it here, anyway. And I'm not going to Biosphere X if that's where you're heading."

"I will return to the Home World to create my Cyber War fighting force. Shortly after, I will come back to Gaea. This time as a conqueror after I have disabled their technology infrastructure. Earth will already be a shambles. Gaea will soon follow and then more targets. Caleb Cassowary will rise from being a Biosphere X Chancellor to Subjugator of the Multiverse. Cosmic Chaos will reign supreme."

"All right, Byzz, if you're coming, let's get ready. Here is my portable quantum motion system. Enter the coordinates for one of Earth's geostationary GPS satellites. It doesn't matter which. There's 24 of them. I can use any one of them to destroy the Control Segment on Earth. That in turn will obliterate the entire satellite array. Earth will come to a disastrous halt. Whole sectors of their global society will self-destruct. That Bear and Horse among them. It's all carefully planned and ready for execution. Help me into this ridiculous spacesuit. You can carry the weapon."

The struggle to get him suited up would have been laughable if it were not so ominous. She slipped into her own suit. He didn't notice the small laser gun she had stowed in the pocket within easy reach. As each moment passed, Byzantia's resolve to kill him off increased. It had to be in space where there would be no hope of rescue or rehab. Permanent annihilation.

She thought, "OK, Caleb, let's go. I'm going to save the Cosmos." She entered the string of numbers in the quantum device and handed it back to him. He connected it to the suit's belt. The unit would propel him to the target satellite. She, being an Adept, would tag along on her own power.

They checked their oxygen supplies. More than enough for the journey. He gave the laser weapon a short test blast and handed it to her. She could have disassembled him right there but there would be explanations required and possible incarceration. Better to wait till they got into space.

He touched the Start button on the Multiverse unit. A short pause and then a low pitched whine and they both disappeared.

In what seemed like only a few seconds, they were standing on the outstretched vanes of a GPS satellite. The equipment itself was in a large box-like container with a dish antenna mounted on top. A legend was painted on the side – US Air Force GPS Satellite Number 14 – and a string of numbers. probably its serial and activation date.

Caleb's voice crackled in her helmet. "Stay here! I have to reach inside the apparatus and make a few adjustments. That will send the fatal signal to the Control system on Earth and the self-destruct process will begin. There's no stopping it once it begins. Then I will blast this unit so the changes I made can't be traced. He crawled over the vane and reached for the container."

Byzz shouted into the intercom. "Caleb, Wait! There's a problem!"

"What problem? How do you know anything about this?

"I don't!" She fired her small gun at the Multiverse device on his belt, disintegrating it. He looked at her in amazement. But not for long. She fired the large weapon several times directly at him. His suit tore apart and exploded with the onrush of escaping oxygen. She thought she heard him scream but couldn't be sure. The blast carried his body or what was left of it off the satellite and sent it spinning through the void. She watched as it rotated away getting smaller by the moment. So much for the great Caleb Cassowary, ex-Chancellor of Biosphere X; ex CTO of the UUI Hexagon; and putative ruler of the Multiverse. Cosmic Chaos averted! She ditched the large weapon.

She looked around. The satellite hummed away unharmed and so did the Earth unknowing of how close it came to destruction. Now, back to land and her unknown fate. She decided to take on the Great Bear. Let's see what his reaction will be and whether he'll keep his promises. That FBI Agent was pretty formidable but that Australian Inspector seemed reasonable enough. She doubted they'd cite her for murder. She had stopped a major catastrophe from happening. More than one, if Caleb had returned to Biosphere X. Could those birds mount a Cyber War? Who knows. And just maybe she could return to the Hex. She had some wonderful new ideas for enhancing the Ursulas. "OK, Here goes. Look out. Shetlands! Byzz is on her way."

Epilogue

Cosmic Chaos averted? Who knows?
One threat's lost out in space, I suppose.
But you never can tell
Where a new one will jell,
As we bring this long tail to a close.

An alarm sounded in the Polar Paradise Secure Multiverse Research Center. The on-duty technician ran to the landing room where a diminutive figure in a light blue space suit had crashed onto the padded floor. She was still in her helmet and holding a laser pistol in her paw. Byzz had returned to Bearmoral Castle.

The tech got on his phone and called Wyatt. "Colonel, we have an invader in the center. Armed and in a space suit, no less. I think it's a female. What should I do?"

"I think I know who it is. If so, she's OK. Hold her there but no rough stuff. We'll be down in just a few minutes."

Wyatt hurried into the Lounge where, as usual, the Octavians were gathered and signaled to Octavius, Bruce, Otto and me. "We have a visitor! In the Research Center. Come on Ursula."

"I leapt to my feet as did Bruce. *(So what else is new? He always leaps)* Otto zapped out to the elevator and summoned a car. Octavius struggled to his feet and waved Chita and Belinda back. "Possible danger, ladies. I'll call you."

Lord David, Dan and Jack looked on curiously over their drinks.

We arrived to find the space suited figure sitting on the floor holding a pistol but not pointing it at anyone or anything. She had taken off her helmet. It was Byzz.

Octavius walked up to her and took the gun. "Well, Ms. Bonobo. You're back. No need to wave that weapon around. You're among friends."

She looked up, blinked and said, "But I've used it. I killed Caleb. I've never shot anyone before."

"Caleb's dead? Where is he?"

"What's left of him is soaring among the GPS satellites with a large tear in his space suit. Another piece of space debris."

"Here, let me help you up. Maury, get her something to drink. Byzz, relax for a few minutes and then tell us what happened. He's really dead?"

"He's a tough bird, Octavius, but he needs air like all of us. I put a large hole in him and his suit and it exploded. He suffocated and then floated off. I also destroyed his quantum motion device. What's left isn't going anywhere."

I returned with a small glass of Scotch. (*What else?*) She sipped it, coughed and handed it back. "Thank you. He planned to destroy the Earth's GPS system. He knew how to send a signal from a satellite that would cripple the system's control segment and knock out the entire array. GPS would be a hulk and Earth's timing and positioning would be hopelessly compromised. His revenge. He also thought it would keep you all busy and deter you from pursuing him when he went back to Biosphere X. That was just step one. He had a whole Cosmic Cyber Campaign planned out. Crazy to the end."

"What was he going to do on Biosphere X?"

"He had major plans to upgrade their ability to wage Cyber Warfare. He got himself set up as Chancellor to the new Protector. He left them with instructions for increasing their capabilities. I don't know whether they can pull it off now that he's gone."

"We'll need to find out. Otto, seems you're going to make another trip. Get us a status report and then 'zap' out of there."

The Otter shrugged. There went my promise to send him somewhere nice. It's a shame Howard or the Colonel couldn't 'zap.'

Bruce looked at her. "In Caleb's permanent absence, I think we can close down this episode. We may want to send an excursion up to search for his body. As far as Interpol is concerned, you're free. I think the FBI will agree.

Ursula 12 had been listening to all of this. She rang her chime. "I've informed Condo about your return and Caleb's demise. He wants to talk with you. Something about getting Ursula 13 off the deck."

(We never told Preston what really happened to Caleb.)

The End - Volume 14 -The Case of Cosmic Chaos

About the Author

Harry DeMaio is a ***nom de plume*** of Harry B. DeMaio, successful author of several books on Information Security and Business Networks as well as the fourteen-volume ***Casebooks of Octavius Bear.*** He is also a published author for Belanger Books and the MX Sherlock Holmes series edited by David Marcum.

A retired business executive, former consultant, information security specialist, private pilot, disk jockey and graduate school adjunct professor, he whiles away his time traveling and writing preposterous books, articles and stories.

He has appeared on many radio and TV shows and is an accomplished, frequent public speaker.

Former New York City natives, he and his extremely patient and helpful wife, Virginia, live in Cincinnati (and several other parallel universes.) They have two sons, living in Scottsdale, Arizona and Cortlandt Manor, New York, both of whom are quite successful and quite normal, thus putting the lie to the theory that insanity is hereditary.

His e-mail is hdemaio@zoomtown.com

You can also find him on Facebook.

His website is www.octaviusbearslair.com

His books are available on Amazon, Barnes and Noble, directly from MX Publishing and at other fine bookstores.